ick Barr

the LONGDOGS

LOUISA CROOK

Louisa Crook, Author

Michele Pollock Dalton, Editor & Designer | www.MichelePollockDalton.com
Sketch by *Rick Barr* | www.Barr26.com/artist

This book is a work of fiction. Names, characters, places, and incidents either are products of the author's imagination or are used fictitiously. Any resemblance to actual persons, living or dead, events, or locales is entirely coincidental.

Printed in the United Kingdom
First Printing: April 2021

Dedicated to my pack:

Layla
My stoic, deadpan,
headstrong Sloughi.

Ami
My kind, gentle,
nurturing Saluki.

Brodie
My courageous, indomitable,
carefree Azawakh.

Mia
My cheeky, fearless, feisty
Italian Greyhound.

This isn't walkies, Layla thought. This was something else, and it wasn't good. Watching Lilian pace erratically, Layla tried to figure out the problem. Her human, Lilian, was not happy - she was stressed. Why was Lilian getting food but no beds?

We're not going to the kennels. What is going on? Layla wondered.

Glued to her phone, Lilian ran frantically up and down the stairs. It was happening - her biggest fear was finally realised, and the woman attempted to put together a plan of action.

With shaking hands, Lilian systematically tied Mia, Layla, Ami, and finally Brodie to her body with their leashes. Then she fed more rope in and around their collars before she tied that around her as well. She knotted everything over and over until she was totally enveloped in a tangled mess of rope and leashes.

Usually, when Lilian touched a leash, the whole pack erupted with excitement. Not this time. Instead, the dogs stood still and watched her in silence.

Lilian sounded strange to the canines, and her voice broke when she tried to shout at Tom. Pupils dilated in fear, Lillian's expressive eyes were wide, and her gaze flitted to the animals at her feet.

The level-headed woman was unaccustomed to this level of panic. Tom always told her that things would never get this bad. Yet Lilian never quite managed to take comfort in his words.

In an unstable foreign country with no support system, no family, and only fair-weather friends for company, how could Tom know how bad things might get?

For years a recurring nightmare haunted Lilian. Whenever she told Tom about it, he rolled his eyes and told her to stop being dramatic. Now, that nightmare was a stark reality. And Lilian was utterly terrified, just like in her dream.

The frightened woman carried a bursting rucksack full of water and dog food when she walked out of the house with the dogs tethered and documents in hand. Lilian attempted to look calm, but the effort failed miserably.

The gates at the opposite end of the compound were open for the first time in the three years they'd lived there. Lilian walked slowly through the entrance, giving the dogs the chance to get in step with her. In the near distance, there was a convoy of military helicopters where once there had been an open wasteland. Lilian stopped, took a breath, and thumbed through the documents pressed to her chest.

"Come on," urged Tom.

Hesitantly, Lilian walked on, her breath more laboured with every step. Tom walked a little ahead of her, probably the first time he'd ever walked faster than his speed-stepping wife. Lilian felt sick as she got to the pick-up zone - she couldn't steady the riotous tremors that wracked her body.

"What's going on here?" the Captain asked as she approached. He looked to Tom for an answer, which was understandable as Lilian didn't look the most level-headed of the pair.

Tom stayed silent and looked at Lilian. He knew, for her peace of mind, that his wife needed to explain for herself.

"My, my dogs… they can come too. I mean, they have paperwork. I mean, I do. I have *their* paperwork. It's all up to date… it's all in order. They can come with us…" Lilian explained. She'd planned what to say and how she would say it, but the torrent of words did not resemble her prepared statement.

The Captain paused and looked back at the helpless husband.

Tom's eyes fell to the ground. He never believed this would work.

"Here," Lilian said as she stretched out a clenched hand, offering the flapping papers.

The Captain looked at Lilian, but his gaze skipped over the documents she proffered. "It's not possible, ma'am." His stance changed from mildly inquisitive to dismissive.

Lilian looked into his eyes. "Please, I cannot leave them behind. I will not leave them behind!" She looked down at her nervous pack. It was the first time she'd seen Mia totally uninterested in meeting a new person.

The Captain's demeanour was unchanged. He looked away as he explained his orders - nothing could be done.

Lilian's eyes welled up. "All of their paperwork is up to date. They can come. They will be allowed into Europe with this paperwork. I made sure."

The cold response from the Captain told her all she needed to know. "Remove the dogs."

Lilian stepped backward. She looked at Tom and saw resignation in his face as tears rolled down her own. "That's okay then. I'll stay. I'll stay here with them. I'll figure out other arrangements. You can leave me here. I'll sign whatever you need. A consent form… whatever."

Clutching at straws, Lilian hoped to be enough of a nuisance that the Captain would let her get on the helicopter with the dogs – a ploy that would allow her to deal with the problem at the other end, in safer territory.

"I'm afraid that's not possible, ma'am. I need you to remove the dogs and come with me."

There was no room to reason with the Captain. Lilian gave a last glance at Tom, who fixed his eyes on Ami, his favourite of the pack.

Lilian hadn't stopped her slow backward steps, and she managed to create a little distance between herself and the others. Suddenly, the woman scooped up the smallest dog, Mia, turned on her heel, and made a dash back to the compound. Layla, Ami, and Brodie accommodated the sudden movement as Layla led the dash - pulling Lilian along even faster.

Lilian heard a yell from the Captain and knew she was being pursued, but she didn't know what she should do. Could she get to the gates and close them before the others got to her?

The frantic woman just wanted to get to her car. *Why did I even try to reason with the Captain?* she wondered. Lilian knew it wouldn't work. What a waste of time. She should have driven away with her dogs as soon as the evacuation began. How naive she had been.

Before she had time to finish kicking herself, she felt arms around her, and Lilian fell to the ground. She managed to drop Mia to one side to save the tiny greyhound from being crushed, but Layla, Ami, and Brodie rolled over in the scuffle.

Lilian screamed. "Get off me! Let me check them! Brodie's leg!" She bucked and squirmed and was eventually pulled to her feet, but not released.

In frustration, Lilian dropped into a crouched position, and her dogs cautiously came close. She checked for injuries, paying particular attention to her tri-paw with the weak back leg. Satisfied that they were okay, Lilian had little time to feel relief as she was pulled back to her feet.

Two soldiers attempted to remove the leashes that bound her to the pack. However, Lilian refused to make it easy. Before they left the house, she'd knotted copious amounts of hard rope, and now Lilian refused to stand still. Tom looked on, unsure what to do as his wife wiggled and twisted. Slowly, Lilian resigned herself to the hopeless situation. Tears fell one by one, then streamed down her face as the woman wailed uncontrollably.

As a comfort, Layla reached up and licked Lilian's face. Brodie and Ami watched from nearby, too scared to come close to the commotion.

After the soldiers removed the last of Lilian's physical connection to the pack, the men walked her toward the landing zone. The dogs followed behind, keeping a distance.

"Wait! Wait! Let me say goodbye! At least let me say goodbye!" Lilian pleaded with the two men, who held her with a vice-like grip. They looked at each other and gave a small nod. Lilian turned and crouched again.

Layla, the stoic Sloughi, led the pack to her. She licked Lilian on her mouth, as she'd always done, and Ami pushed her nose in under Lilian's chin. Brodie pushed in between Layla and Ami - the Azawakh's mouth open with his long tongue flopping out at the side as it always did. Lilian pulled them all in close while little Mia crept into her lap and curled up neatly. Red-faced and unable to make eye contact, Tom crouched down as he said his goodbyes to each dog.

Lilian felt sick - she couldn't bear the images that formed in her mind. Her beloved animals wouldn't survive. Leaving the dogs behind was a death sentence, and they would all suffer long, drawn-out, and painful ends.

She got up slowly and turned toward the landing zone - as if to make her way there. Seemingly pleased with Lilian's cooperation, the soldiers loosened their grips and began to walk. Instead, Lilian turned and bolted toward the back of the compound, where there was a hole in the fence.

"Come on! This way! Come on!" she shouted to the dogs. The pack chased after her, as did Tom and the soldiers. Unable to outrun them, the men tackled Lilian to the ground without mercy. The wind was knocked out of her when she slammed into the rubble-covered dirt. As she struggled to get her breath back, Lilian went limp.

"Stop this, Lilian. You can't do anything. Just stop now. You're making it harder," her husband scolded.

Lilian shot a furious look Tom's way. The soldiers dragged her toward the landing zone as she watched the confused hounds trot after them, keeping a distance but never stopping.

A helicopter started up as they approached the landing zone, and the noise stopped Layla dead in her tracks. The others stopped a little way behind their leader, except for Mia – the worried little greyhound jumped at Tom, wanting to be picked up.

Mia wanted to be comforted by her favourite person. But Tom walked away, his gaze everywhere except on his precious little girl. Frightened by the loud noise, Mia stopped – overwhelmed by the situation.

Lilian sobbed as she pleaded with everyone around her to reconsider. Her words fell on deaf ears as she was loaded onto the helicopter. "I'll come back," she mumbled to herself. "I'll come back and find you. I always come back."

As Lilian was strapped into the helicopter, she pushed against the seat-back and felt her rucksack full of dog food and water. She panicked and frantically pulled it off her shoulders. Lilian unzipped it and leaned toward the door, throwing the supplies out just before the door closed.

Lilian didn't know what good the rucksack full of supplies would do. Her dogs were doomed - food would give them a few extra days. The water was in bottles and useless to them. Lilian sobbed at the futility of the gesture. Her sobs became wails as the helicopter rose. She could see her four confused hounds watching, following the helicopter as it moved further and further away. Grief-stricken, she fell silent and closed her eyes.

Silence descended on the four hounds as they kept their necks craned up to the sky. They stood there for some time before Layla broke her gaze and surveyed the area. It was eerily still; there were no people around and no giant metal monsters moving along the roads. Even the birds seemed to have disappeared.

Standing closest to the launch area, Mia was the first to speak. "I don't understand." She trotted back to the group. The others looked at her but didn't say anything.

Ami slowly walked toward Layla, stopping alongside her. "Do you think they're coming back?" she asked as she continued to look up at the sky.

"I don't know, but we're on our own right now," Layla answered.

Ami bowed her head. "What should we tell them?"

Layla looked over at Mia and Brodie, who snuffled around the rucksack Lilian threw from the chopper. "Let's not worry them anymore yet."

Layla walked over to Mia and Brodie just as they'd pulled a bag of food out of the rucksack. "Stop!" she barked.

Brodie and Mia looked up at her with confusion plastered across their faces.

"It's food! It's our food!" exclaimed Mia with glee, as though Layla hadn't noticed the bounty they found.

"Let's see how much there is," Layla answered as she pawed at the rucksack until all of the contents fell out. Four small bags of food, two large bottles of water, and two blankets. It wasn't going to keep them for long. "Let's hide this."

Mia looked at Layla, then at the food. "No, let's eat this!"

Ignoring the little greyhound, Layla picked up the first bag of food and looked at their surroundings. Where could she hide it so that other dogs wouldn't find it?

Ami walked over to Layla and looked around too. "There's going to be strays all around here soon."

Layla nodded. "Wait here." She dropped the bag of food and ran off in the direction of their house. Maybe, just maybe, Lilian left it open.

"Wait here!" Ami admonished as she curtailed Brodie and Mia's instinct to follow Layla.

"But where's she going?" asked Brodie, his focus still on the black Sloughi running toward the compound.

"She's just checking something out; she's not going far," Ami replied.

They heard a bark and saw Layla standing at the gates, looking at them.

"Come on then." Ami led the way to Layla.

The trio joined Layla as she led them back to their home. She pushed the door with her paw, and it opened.

Relieved, Brodie was the first to go inside. He needed to lie down for a while as his weakened back leg was tired and sore. Oblivious to the danger they were in, Brodie went to his favourite spot on the sofa, curled up, and closed his eyes.

"We need to get the food." Layla asserted when she nudged the door open again. With Ami's help, it took two trips to get the bags of food from the rucksack back to the house.

"Water?" Ami looked at the two bowls on the kitchen floor. "That won't last long."

Remembering the bottles that Lilian packed, Layla and Ami returned to the rucksack. They both pawed at the crackling plastic.

"Hopeless," Ami sighed in defeat after tentatively gnawing at the lid. "We can't open these."

Layla looked at the bottles. "Just pick it up; we'll figure something out." Each of the dogs ran back to the house with a bottle clenched in their jaws.

When they returned, Brodie's head was down, but his eyes were open. Mia was on the opposite end of the sofa, in much the same position.

None of them fully understood what happened, but they knew something was horribly wrong. Lilian and Tom left them a few times before, but never like this - never home alone. They went to a different house in the past, or they'd go to a noisy place with pens and other dogs. This was different. This never happened before.

"Don't close the door," Layla warned the others. "We won't be able to get out if you do that."

Mia lifted her head. "Why do we need to go out?"

Layla looked at Mia, unsure of how to answer her question. "Just don't close the door."

Mia seemed to accept Layla's request and rested her chin back on the cushion.

Ami and Layla slowly walked into the kitchen. "We're going to have to tell them something," Ami urged.

Layla spoke quietly, "I know. Let's give it a while though. Let's rest. We need to think about this."

Exhausted, they both walked back to the sofa and curled up with Brodie and Mia. Together there was small comfort, and after a little time, they slept.

* * * * *

Layla woke to the sound of water being lapped up. She lifted her head to see Brodie as he gulped to his heart's content.

"Stop!" she yelled.

Brodie flinched and knocked the bowl, spilling some water over the edge. "What? What's the problem?"

The noise woke Ami up, and she gave Layla an admonishing look. "It's okay, Brodie, you haven't done anything wrong," Ami paused and looked at Layla, who nodded back at her. "We need to talk," Ami suggested.

Ami walked over to Mia, who slept through the commotion, and nudged her awake.

Startled, Mia bolted up as she always did. "What is it? Are they back?" She jumped down from the sofa and trotted around.

The big brown Saluki was gentle in her response. "No, Mia, they're not back. We need to have a talk now. Come back here," Ami softly encouraged.

Ami moved to the sofa while Layla followed and sat beside her. Mia and Brodie sat on the opposite sofa, facing the two meeting-callers.

"We don't know what happened, but it doesn't look good. This wasn't planned. You saw how Lilian acted. She didn't mean to leave us. She didn't want to leave us." Ami tried her best to be calm with her delivery, but the lump in her throat got larger and larger with every utterance.

Layla took over. "Look, we're on our own now. We have to find our own food and water, which means we can't drink willy-nilly like we're used to doing. Okay, Brodie?" she questioned with a tone lightly tinged with accusation.

Brodie hung his head. "I didn't know; I didn't think…"

"Well, start thinking. Think about everything you do now," Layla harshly reprimanded.

When Ami shot Layla a glance that said, "rein it in," Layla spoke with more care: "We just need to make some rules for now, okay?"

Mia had trouble digesting the information. "What do you mean 'we're on our own?' We're not. They'll come back. They always come back."

Layla had no choice but to state the obvious. "Whenever they've left us, they've taken us somewhere, remember? We go to the big cages, or we go to stay at another house, or someone comes here. None of that happened. Think about it."

Layla's words stung, but the reality of their situation was apparent.

"So what then? What do we do now?" Mia's eyes rested on Layla and stayed there, burning into her.

"I don't know. I need to think about this," Layla announced, and the meeting was over.

The house felt weird after Layla's words. Being there felt uncomfortable, and it put them all on edge. This had been their home – a safe place and a sanctuary - but now it felt creepy and unwelcome.

Layla didn't know if staying was the right decision, but she needed time to think. If nothing else, the house provided shelter from the scorching temperatures outside. It wouldn't last long, but there was some water, and the food Lilian left in the rucksack.

Suddenly, Layla jumped up and ran to the kitchen, and the others instinctively followed. The curious trio found Layla in front of the green bin where Lilian kept some of their food. If they could get into it, it would buy them time to find more food elsewhere.

Without a word, they all knew what they needed to do. Brodie hopped forward and nudged the bin with his nose. "It's full," he exclaimed in relief as he glanced at the others.

The container, slotted snuggly into a large shelf, presented a challenge. So, as the pack's bin raiding expert, Ami walked over and nudged the lid open. There was only an inch of clearance, not nearly enough for them to get to the food. "We need to get the bin out of there," she sighed. The shelf unit was against the wall, so there was no chance of getting behind it to push. "We're going to have to pull it off the shelf," Ami sighed.

It wouldn't be easy; there was only a slight lip to the bin, so getting any purchase on it would be difficult. Ami clamped onto the lip of the container as firmly as she could and pulled. "Ugh!" she exclaimed, as she lost her grip and stumbled backward.

"Let me try," said Brodie. He'd felt pretty useless up until now. He hadn't helped with anything and still felt guilty about drinking so much of their water.

Without comment, Layla and Ami looked at each other as their three-legged pack member hopped forward. Equipped with the narrowest snout of the three larger dogs, Brodie wedged his bottom teeth under the ridge of the lip of the bin and got ready to pull.

"Go on, Brodie, you can do it!" Ami encouraged her friend, though she had little faith he could accomplish the task.

Searching the kitchen for some other solution, Layla was less subtle in expressing her doubt. But her interest focused on Brodie when she heard a scrape, and she looked back to find the bin pulled out by a few inches.

Brodie shrugged and yanked to wrestle the bin out, and with a few more tugs, it was free. The container crashed down onto its side, the lid flew off, and the contents spilled onto the kitchen floor.

Brodie shook his head. His jaw hurt a little, but his pride helped dull the pain. He smiled at the others, his gaze pinned on Layla, who gave him a slight but meaningful nod.

"Well done, Brodie!" Ami was elated, both at what Brodie accomplished and at the prospect of meals to come.

"We still have to be sparing." Layla's voice of reason brought the celebrations to a swift end. They knew she was right. "From now on, we only eat when we feel really hungry. No gorging. Just eat enough to take the edge off. We don't know how long this needs to last us."

Mia looked at the floor and mumbled, "I'm hungry now." Her eyes flicked up just long enough to see if Layla heard her.

"Are you really hungry, or do you just want to eat?" Layla questioned.

The others were well aware of Mia's insatiable appetite. She was one-third their size but could eat more than all of them put together.

"I really am hungry. Please just a few," the little dog pleaded.

Layla nodded and gave her a look that told her not to take advantage. It took everything Mia had in her not to disobey.

"What about water?" Ami pawed at the plastic bottles Lilian threw from the helicopter.

As Mia relinquished any responsibility for their welfare, Layla assumed the greyhound's place as the pack leader. But she felt defeated. "I don't know how to get it out of there."

Trying to help, Brodie suggested, "We can chew through it." But his lack of foresight was apparent.

Layla briskly dismissed his suggestion. "And when it spreads out all over the floor? What then? We'll get a few licks, and it'll be gone. We need to find water from a different place."

Layla walked to the bathroom, and Brodie proudly took the opportunity to demonstrate his knowledge of the toilet-bowl. "You can't drink that blue water. Tastes disgusting."

With a look of subtle disapproval on her generally stoic face, Layla gazed at Brodie. Then she walked over to the shower tap. They'd all been rinsed off in the shower countless times after a beach run. Why, oh, why hadn't she looked just once at how they made the water come? "We need to push something. We need to make the water run."

Layla jumped up beside the tap and put her front paws against the wall on either side of it. She pushed her nose against the handle. It moved! Hopeful, she nudged it to the left - nothing. Layla readjusted her position and moved it back over, all the way to the right – still nothing. She dropped back down to all fours, and Layla could feel three sets of eyes as they burned into her back. Ignoring the sensation, Layla jumped up once more and nudged the tap handle up. The Sloughi excitedly jumped backward when a blast of water hit her.

"Yes! You did it! Well done, Layla!" Ami was delighted, and the others echoed her relief.

Layla rarely showed excitement, but this was enough to make her drop her indomitable composure for a moment. "Drink up! We don't have to ration this. It doesn't stop coming."

And they all drank until their bellies swelled.

* * * * *

Darkness fell on the compound, and the euphoric sense of victory subsided. The pack retired to their normal places on the sofas in the upstairs lounge. No one spoke about how strange it felt with Lilian and Tom absent. In fact, no one spoke at all. They all felt a deep sense of loss.

Every night, as long as they lived there, they would all bunker down with their human pack members - to watch movies, to enjoy belly rubs and ear scratches, to beg for morsels of food – wholly safe and loved.

Finding comfort in each other helped the pack relax, but an unsettled and uncertain future disquieted them. The group existed in a perpetual state of uneasiness for three days, sleeping long hours to stave off hunger for as long as they could.

After day one, the biscuits went stale. On day four, Layla ate her allocated ration, then announced, "We've got one day of food left."

The blow hit hard, and morale, low as it was, bottomed out.

Ami, who struggled with the meagre food portions, questioned, "Well, what do we do now?" The sturdy second-in-command panicked, and Ami's voice broke as she whined and paced.

"Calm down, I'll think of something."

Ami picked up on the lack of conviction in Layla's utterance and refused to calm down.

Layla continued to placate her best friend. "We have water. That's the most important thing. We haven't looked for food outside of this house. Let's go. All of us. Let's search the other houses."

Ami's ears pricked up. Layla was right. Maybe other houses would have food - lots of food. The pack headed downstairs toward the front door, which still stood ajar. Mia pushed her tiny snout into the gap and nudged the door open enough for everyone to get through. It was a strange pack-focused gesture from the usually self-centered dog.

Layla delivered the plan. "Okay, let's spread out. We'll take a street each. Don't get trapped inside. When you find a house with an open door, mark it, and move on. Do not go inside on your own. Remember, some of these houses may have dogs. We'll meet back at our place."

The pack nodded in unison and spread out with almost military-like coordination. Brodie took the street they were on, Mia the next, Ami the one after that, and Layla bolted to the furthest row of houses.

Four houses down, and Mia still hadn't found an open one. She moved quickly, pushing each door firmly with a two-paw shove. After all the houses on one side of the street were done, she started on the other side. A sinking feeling grew in the pit of her stomach. Just two more houses left.

"Come on," Mia pleaded with the door in front of her. She took a deep breath, jumped up, and pressed her front paws against it. It swung open, and Mia stumbled forward, not ready for it to give way so easily. "Yes!" she squealed, delighted and relieved.

"No, no, no!" Mia's elation quickly disappeared as she watched the door swing back and latch shut. She stood completely still, looking at the house in disbelief. Utterly deflated, Mia walked past the final house, without so much as a glimpse at the door.

She got a few metres away before Mia stopped and turned to look back at it. With a heavy sigh, she trotted over and pawed dismissively at the door. It moved. It wasn't locked. "Thank goodness!"

Mia perked up immediately and slid carefully through the gap in the door, completely forgetting Layla's instructions. The house smelled funny, but it was a smell Mia encountered before. She couldn't recall where though. Mia stepped cautiously through the house, finally recalling Layla's words. As it so often did, Mia's curiosity got the better of her.

As Mia walked further into the house, she couldn't smell any food or dogs. *Maybe this is a human-only home,* she thought. Mia knew many people didn't like her kind.

With nothing of interest downstairs, Mia moved to the second floor. Overwhelmed by a sense of being watched, Mia suddenly felt very afraid and very alone.

The acidic smell grew stronger, and the dog's eyes widened. She realised where she smelled it before! Frantic, Mia turned and fled down the stairs as fast as she could go. Before she got to the last step, the greyhound felt something dart past her. When she looked to the door, Mia saw what she feared and stopped dead.

Raven was well known throughout the compound - she was abnormally large compared to other cats' delicate frames. She wasn't fat; she was built - a large body with long, thick limbs. The feline had a dominating presence, and she knew it. There wasn't a single cat or dog that messed with Raven twice. Her fearsome reputation for cruelty was often displayed when another animal crossed her path.

Mia was half Raven's size, and the tiny greyhound was scared. She watched Raven saunter casually back and forth in front of the door that Mia desperately wanted to be on the other side of.

"What are you doing here, little dog?" Raven didn't bother to look at the quivering grey intruder as she casually began her inquisition.

"I... I'm sorry. I was just going."

Raven's eyes moved to focus on Mia, looking her up and down. "Well, that doesn't answer my question, does it?" Raven taunted as she continued to circle in front of the door, her tail swishing every few steps.

"Everyone's gone. I was, I was looking for food. We don't have much left. I'm sorry. I didn't know this was your house."

Raven smiled as she looked at Mia. "Of *course* this is my house. They're all my houses now."

The dread in Mia's stomach built. She had no idea how to get out of the situation. "Facing Raven in close quarters is not a good idea," Mia whimpered under her breath. Overwhelmed by regret, the greyhound clenched her teeth as she wished she'd listened to Layla. "If you just let me go, I'll be on my way. I won't bother you again, I promise."

At this, Raven stopped and sat down in the door gap. She nonchalantly groomed herself, claws flexed, as she licked her paws and rubbed behind her ears.

Mia looked at the bright-white talons that extended from the jet-black fur. Nervously, she shuffled backward.

Claws unfurled in front of her face; Raven ordered, "Stay where you are!"

Mia froze, and Raven retracted the weapons that blinded many an adversary. Then the intimidating feline carried on grooming.

Mia drew an audible breath when Ami's voice sounded in the distance. She'd been gone some time, and now, Mia's friends searched for her. The greyhound's heart sank as she remembered that she never marked the house. How would they ever find her? *Why can't I ever just follow instructions?* she silently fussed.

"Where are you?" Layla called, and this time the Sloughi was close.

Mia thought quickly. She had to let them know where she was before they got out of earshot. "Layla! I'm here! He..." Before Mia could finish the word, Raven pounced. Mia screamed as she felt teeth sink into her flesh and claws drag across her skin. She kicked as hard as she could, but Mia couldn't free herself from the feline's rage. Raven was just too strong, too big. Still screaming, Mia rolled across the floor, desperate to shake Raven off. She was no match for the cat, but she wouldn't submit easily. Mia bucked and flipped as she felt the skin tear along her belly. She flailed her head from side to side as Raven attempted to slash at her eyes.

Wide-eyed and panicked, Ami yelled, "Where is it coming from? Where is she?"

The trio of dogs ran frantically up and down the road, searching for another clue to lead them to Mia.

"Shhh!" Layla hushed Ami as she tried to place the next scream. "Just push all the doors. Go!"

Mia finally managed to get purchase with one of her bites, and she clamped down as hard as she could. Raven screeched and backed off.

Wincing in pain, Mia stood. Blood ran down her legs and dripped onto the floor, but she didn't take her eyes off Raven. She didn't need to see the injuries to know she was badly hurt.

The cat swished her tail angrily and hissed at Mia. "Pretty good for a warm-up," Raven taunted as she smiled at her prey. The cat backed up, prepared to pounce again. Mia crouched and screamed as the huge black cat bolted toward her.

"Mia!" Layla burst through the door, clipping Raven's back legs and sending her off-course.

"Layla! Help me!" Mia limped over to the protective black Sloughi.

Standing tall in the doorway, Layla focused on the furious feline. Her skin crawled - there was nothing in the world that Layla hated more than cats. "Get out, Mia," Layla directed.

Slowly, Mia shuffled out of the house, every step in agony.

"I know you!" hissed Raven as she arched her back and puffed up her fur.

"Likewise," Layla replied with vitriol. The two held their stares for a moment - until Brodie broke the silence with a less than stealthy entry into the house.

Instinctively, the muscular Azawakh moved to attack the cat in front of Layla.

"No, Brodie!" commanded his leader and friend.

Brodie stopped but didn't take his eyes off Raven.

"Did you see what she did? Did you see Mia?" Brodie glared at Raven, who hadn't taken her eyes off Layla, despite darting backward when Brodie advanced.

"Yes, I saw. Let's go. Let's go, Brodie! Brodie? Brodie! Get out!" Layla kept her eyes on Raven as Brodie reluctantly turned to leave. The tri-paw couldn't step backward very quickly because of his semi-functional hind leg, so Layla carefully watched his retreat. Once Brodie was out, Layla cautiously withdrew, eyes fixed on Raven until she was clear of the house.

Breathing heavily and whimpering, Mia stretched out in the street. Ami and Brodie frantically licked the blood that poured from the little dog's wounds.

Ami stopped for a moment to look up at Layla. Neither of them said anything, though Ami knew Layla wanted to scold the little grey dog to within an inch of her life. Ami's expression made sure their pack leader knew it was not the time.

"How bad is it?" Layla solemnly asked the two dogs that worked to clean Mia up.

Panicked, Ami replied, "I don't know. There's just so much blood. Her stomach…"

Layla looked at the shredded flesh on Mia's underside. "Cats," she growled as she looked back at the house.

Ami sensed Layla's thoughts and intervened: "We need to get her home. Mia, can you walk?"

Wobbly, Mia slowly stood up and took a few steps. With a nod at Ami, Mia carefully made her way toward their street.

Hopping one step for every few steps Mia made, Brodie stayed beside his injured friend.

Ami dropped back to talk to Layla. "Mia's badly hurt. She's lost so much blood. That tiny body…" Ami's eyes welled up. Though her puppies were long gone, Ami never lost her strong maternal instinct.

"She has to rest and eat. There's nothing else we can do," Layla replied.

The pair walked on as they reflected on the problems they faced. During their search, the pack scoured the entire compound and found three open homes, four if they included Raven's lair. Now they had to go back and see if they could find food inside any of them.

If the little greyhound hoped to make a recovery, the larger dogs would have to sacrifice their rations to Mia unless they could find more food.

Layla shouted to Brodie up ahead. "Bro! Get her settled and resting. We're going to search the open houses."

Brodie looked back with a horrified expression and shook his head.

"We'll be fine. It's not going to happen to us. We're smarter than that," Layla remarked.

Mia heard the jibe from the black Sloughi but didn't react. She was in too much pain to protest. She just wanted to get home, curl up, and sleep.

Reluctantly, Brodie turned back and escorted his injured pack member home.

"We'll be as quick as we can," Ami reassured. Then the motherly Saluki shot a glance at Layla. "That wasn't necessary."

Layla frowned at Ami. "She didn't listen, did she? She went inside, by herself, and look what happened. We're in enough trouble. We don't need more."

Ami knew Layla was right. Mia never did as she was told. The tiny Italian greyhound was Lilian and Tom's first dog, and she was the centre of their world for two years until Layla arrived. So, Mia acted like the rules didn't apply to her and that she was better than the others.

"She'll learn from this, if she lives."

Ami's ears pricked up at the callous way Layla spoke. She trotted on to the first house they marked. Layla followed behind, on constant watch for other feline foes.

When they got to the first house, they entered slowly and cautiously. It smelled of the stuff Lilian washed the floors with, but stronger. It stung their eyes and made it hard to catch any scent that might lead them to food.

"Just the kitchen. There won't be food anywhere else."

Ami nodded compliantly. The pair quickly moved through the room. There wasn't a single morsel to be found. They stretched up to look at the counters, and still nothing. They couldn't pick up on any animal smells.

"There's nothing here, next house." Layla led the way out of the home.

They both took a deep breath when they got outside, trying to clear their noses of the acrid smell of disinfectant.

The pair moved quickly on to the next marked house. Immediately Ami found a small loaf of bread on a countertop. She grabbed it and smiled at Layla, a little too elated for the tiny amount of food. Layla scratched at the cupboard door, frustrated that she couldn't get into them. She knew that's where the food would be.

"We've tried so many times. It's not possible," Ami tried to comfort her defeated friend. They tried over and over in their own home to get the cupboards open and never managed it.

Discouraged, they left with the lone loaf and moved to the final house. Ami dropped the bread just inside the door and found Layla already with her head inside the furthest cupboard.

"It was open!" Layla excitedly shouted as she felt Ami approach.

Remembering how many of the low cupboards at their house contained things to cook with instead of things to cook, Ami asked, "And it's food? It's not those funny bowls?"

Layla backed out of the cupboard and turned to Ami, throwing a bag of pasta at the Saluki's feet. They both looked down at the minuscule bounty.

Never one to dwell on disaster, Ami led Layla out of the house, where she picked up the loaf of bread. Then they hurried home to their friends.

* * * * *

Mia hadn't made it to her favourite spot on the desk upstairs where Lilian worked. Instead, she curled up on the downstairs sofa. And Mia's forehead wrinkled up every time Brodie licked her. "He's too rough." The injured greyhound looked expectantly at Ami as soon as she entered the room, deflating the well-meaning tri-paw.

Ami smiled at Brodie as she walked over and continued his work.

"That's all?" Brodie looked at the meagre bounty. "All of that work, all of this, for that?" He looked over at Mia and then at Layla.

"We had to try." Layla pushed past Brodie and took her place on the sofa to rest. She refused to tackle the subject of food anymore. She knew they would all have to give up their rations for Mia to get better.

"I think she's stopped bleeding." Ami looked over at Layla.

"Then rest now," Layla gently ordered.

The exhausted pack quickly fell into an uneasy sleep.

Three days after Mia's attack, she surprised the others with her quick recovery: she trotted about by the end of the second day and ran up and down the stairs by the third.

Mia may have felt better, but her body looked awful. The tears and rips in her flesh created huge bloody scabs, and they pulled her skin in strange ways as she moved.

Layla didn't voice it, but she was impressed with how well the little dog coped.

Ami stayed quiet during Mia's recuperation. The motherly Saluki gave her rations to Mia, just as the others had. Resigned, she crunched her way through the dry pasta and nibbled on the measly portion of bread. But Ami was utterly miserable. "I'm so hungry."

"Me too," whined Brodie. He struggled terribly with the food situation. He didn't like pasta, and he didn't care for bread. "We're going to starve."

Brodie's words cut through them all. Mia had felt a little guilty for taking their biscuit rations, but at that moment, she felt truly awful. "Layla? What do we do?"

Layla looked at Mia but stayed silent.

Ami could see there was something Layla was pondering. "What? What is it?" the gentle dog questioned.

Until Ami asked, Layla silently considered an awful option but refused to voice it - for fear she might have to see the idea through. "The house where Mia was attacked."

All eyes swiveled to Layla.

With concern in her gentle voice, Ami asked, "What about it?"

"Cats live there, right? Well, at least one cat?" Layla rhetorically asked.

"No kidding!" Mia blurted.

Layla paused, and Mia dropped her gaze, indicating she wouldn't interrupt again.

"Well, then there must be cat food in there. Did you see any, Mia?"

Ashamed, Mia hung her head. She'd gotten herself into serious trouble, taken her friends' rations, and she hadn't even discovered if the house had food in it.

The conclusion obvious; Layla didn't wait for Mia's answer. The unspoken admonishment settled on their disobedient little pack member.

Most dogs dislike cats, but Layla didn't just dislike them - she found them repulsive! And though the thought of returning to the cat's house made her feel nauseous, Layla muttered, "We've got to go back there." And she almost choked on the words.

"Are you all nuts?" Mia asked when she realised no one else questioned the Sloughi's statement.

"What choice do we have?" Ami looked at Mia and then back at Layla. "Let's do it. She won't touch us if we both go."

Brodie stood up and hopped forward. "If all three of us go."

Seeing how eager he was to seek approval from his pack leader, Layla nodded.

Brodie looked proud, as though he had been selected, rather than volunteered himself. He hopped to the front door, ready to go.

Ami smiled affectionately at him and looked at Layla, as if to thank her for humouring the roan-coloured Azawakh. She walked over to Mia, who stared at them all in disbelief. "Don't worry. We'll be fine. Raven's not going to attack the three of us. She wouldn't dare." Ami tried to reassure the disheveled dog. She turned and walked to the door to meet Brodie as he nudged it open, Layla following behind.

"What if there's more than one?" Mia called as they exited the house.

For a split second, Layla stopped in her tracks. The stoic Sloughi already considered that possibility. But she managed to tame the fear of running into more than one disgusting feline in that house, at least until Mia shined a light on the horrific prospect.

* * * * *

The three hounds stood side by side outside the house, looking at the door they were about to enter. As usual, Layla briefed the others. "Same drill, okay, Ami? In, straight to the kitchen, grab whatever you can find, and then get out. Brodie, you follow us and be on guard. Stay close to us. Really close."

Brodie sternly nodded, and the trio tentatively moved forward.

After a quick look at the two tense hounds, Layla pushed against the door until it was wide open and stayed open. The cautious leader didn't want anything to hinder a quick retreat.

Layla shuddered as the stench of feline hit her nose. "Why would anyone want cats in their house?" the Sloughi muttered as she cautiously headed to the kitchen, with Ami and Brodie close behind.

After he paused and scanned the kitchen, Brodie took his position in the doorway. The tri-paw was relieved he didn't find any lurking moggies.

"Right, come on. Let's get this done quick," the lead dog commanded as she and Ami started to rummage through everything within reach.

"Jackpot!" Ami excitedly exclaimed as she pulled out a full bag of cat biscuits.

"Shhhhh!" The fear that they'd encounter Raven barred Layla's participation in Ami's excitement. After a last, quick look around, the hounds prepared to retreat. "Let's g—"

Layla turned as Brodie slowly backed into the kitchen, his eyes fixed on something in front of him. He was silent, so the others followed suit. Layla moved as close to the Azawakh as she could get.

Brodie whispered, but didn't break his gaze, "I saw something."

A chill ran down Layla's spine. She moved her head close to Brodie's and focused on the point that drew his attention. Sure enough, two bright dots gazed back at them.

Trying not to rustle the bag of kibble hanging from her teeth, Ami stayed utterly still.

The front door laid straight before them – an easy dash from the kitchen.

"We've got to run together. That cat is not going to take on three dogs." Layla didn't sound as sure as usual, but her two friends didn't seem to notice. "Ami, you go first, then you, Brodie. I'll take up the rear. On my count."

As they assumed their positions, Brodie let out an almost inaudible growl. When Layla looked toward the door, she spotted Raven – the despised animal haughtily blocked their exit. Raven looked at them with bold disdain, and Layla's blood boiled at the sight of the arrogant feline.

How dare she! How dare she think that she can intimidate us! Layla thought as she lost her composure. The headstrong leader charged the giant black cat that sat between them and their escape.

Raven's eyes widened with surprise, and before she had a chance to back up, she felt the black dog's long snout dig under her belly.

Layla threw her head up high, tossing Raven clear into the next room. If she hadn't hit the sofa on her way down, the cat would have landed on her feet. Dazed and aghast, Raven shook her head while Layla stood, all four paws grounded, ready for retaliation. Ami and Brodie watched in horror.

"Go!" a muffled voice yelled at Brodie. Ami bumped him with the bag of kibble she still held in her jaws, and they both bolted out of the kitchen and through the front door.

Layla wasted no time and followed the pair as they ran home elated.

After bursting through the front door, the hounds eagerly clamoured to show Mia their bounty. But she wasn't downstairs, so they headed up to the second level. They found the little greyhound with her worried gaze locked on the bathroom.

"What? What is it?"

Mia looked at Layla and nodded toward the tap. "It's stopped."

Enthusiasm obliterated; the previously victorious trio peered at the bowl they'd slid into the shower to catch the water. The anti-climactic moment came when they realised silence replaced the sound of running water.

An all too familiar sense of unease swept over them.

Crestfallen, Layla stated the obvious. "We'd better make that last then."

Interrupting the lingering quiet, Ami attempted to lift spirits with a hopeful reminder: "At least we have more food."

Uninterested in a morale boost, Layla scoffed, "We need water more than we need food." Devastated, she shuddered as she remembered the feel of cat hair on her face! "We went to such an effort to get more food only to run out of water," she growled to herself.

A few more minutes of silence passed before Brodie spoke up, "She really went flying." He looked at Ami, who smiled back.

Then they both looked at Layla. She saw their grins and couldn't help but giggle a little.

"She really did! Did you see the look on her face?" added Ami.

Layla's giggle turned into a full belly laugh, and the rest of her pack quickly joined the merriment. Mia made Ami and Brodie tell her the story of their valiant escape three times, and each time she squealed in glee when Ami described the "flying feline" part.

Relieved that Mia was in good spirits and recovering well, Layla found the little dog's reaction quite adorable. The two hounds rarely saw eye-to-eye, but Mia was part of her pack, and that meant something.

The laughter soon died down as the group faced reality - two days of water and a bag of cat kibble wouldn't last them long.

It was getting late, so Layla suggested an evening meal, a little water, and then sleep. They all agreed and went one by one to get their rations. They snuggled up just a little closer to one another on the sofa downstairs and fell into a deep slumber.

Layla's eyes opened while it was still dark, and she wondered why she was awake. Normally she slept until the light started to break through the windows, so she closed her eyes to go back to sleep. But they didn't stay closed for long. Before she could drop off again, Layla heard a noise, and she wondered, *Where is it coming from?*

Eyes wide open, Layla stayed still while she attempted to scan the darkness. *There it is again! The kitchen. It's coming from the kitchen,* she thought. Straining to hear the noises, Layla stood and slowly crept forward. Her dark fur stood on end when she realised the situation: she might be a sighthound, but when it came to cat-talk, she never missed a beat. She could hear feline voices and the crunch of kibble.

Layla crept back and nudged Ami awake, then nodded for Ami to prick up her ears.

The Saluki tilted her head, and her eyes widened as she recognized the sounds.

Layla and Ami shared a meaningful look before they nodded in agreement. They moved in silence as Layla nudged Brodie awake. Ami tried to rouse Mia, who always slept a bit further away.

Brodie woke to Layla's stern expression and understood he must stay quiet. He got up, stretched out his bad hip, and stood behind the Sloughi.

Ami nudged Mia ever so gently. No response. She nudged the greyhound again, and the little dog still didn't stir.

With the third nudge, Mia shot up with a yelp. "What? What is it?" she shouted.

"Shhhhhh! Be quiet!" Ami tried to hush the noisiest member of their pack, but it was too late. As soon as Mia shouted, they heard claws scrabble and kitchen utensils fall.

"Go, go, get out!" Layla yelled as she bumped Brodie to lead the way. Ami followed suit and pushed a bewildered Mia after him, forcefully nudging her the whole way.

Layla bolted for the door as soon as the others were clear. On the front steps, the big black dog screamed in pain as she felt two sets of claws dig into her thigh. She turned and saw the fiery, angry eyes of Raven as she opened her mouth to clamp down. Layla kicked out her back legs and sent Raven airborne.

"Run!" Layla called to the pack as she shot past them and through the gates of the compound. The Sloughi didn't stop until she reached a small open space by another residential complex.

Smiling in excitement, Brodie yelled, "That was close!"

Layla wasn't quite so amused. "Bloody cats!" she fumed.

Dopey and confused, Mia asked, "Is that what it was?" The petite dog didn't expect an answer, and she really didn't care. Still sleepy, she found a soft patch of dirt and curled up.

Though her insides twisted with worry, Ami attempted to placate Layla. "We couldn't have stayed there much longer anyway. No food, no water…"

Layla glanced at Ami's sympathetic face, at the tiny dog curled up in the dirt, and then at the amused, hopeful boy settled next to her. The stoic lady snapped out of her moment of rage and thought hard. They needed food, water, and somewhere to stay out of the torrid heat. "Before Lilian and Tom took us in, do you remember getting water from the grass?"

Ami knew what Layla meant. In the past, the two were the only ones forced to survive on the streets, and those street smarts were vital for the hounds' future. Ami reminded her friend, "The next compound! There's loads of grass outside it."

Layla remembered. Shortly after her rescue, she ran away from Lilian and Tom. Layla felt a pang of guilt when she recalled how Lilian cried when they found her there, lazing on the grass.

"Wake her up," Layla motioned to Mia as she took off in the direction of the next housing complex.

"What now?" Mia protested. "I just want to sleep!" She'd never been good at waking up early.

When they arrived, a deflated Brodie scratched at the scorched grass beneath his paws. "I guess the water stopped here too."

"What now, Layla?" Mia asked the question, but all three dogs looked to their leader.

"We keep looking." The Sloughi led them back the way they'd come;

she remembered a large building in front of their compound. There were people there all the time, so maybe there would be water too. "Yes!" Layla couldn't conceal her pride as she led her pack to the flower bed, where spurts of water trickled out of black tubes.

"This is going to take forever," Mia whined.

Ami nudged her in admonishment. "Even longer if you keep talking."

The greyhound wasn't wrong. It took a long time to quench the hounds' thirst, but they persisted until their bellies rounded. Replete, the pack stretched out in the early morning sun, and for a few minutes, they all felt at ease. Then they slept.

* * * * *

"Go! Yah!" The dogs woke in a panic. Two angry humans charged the animals, wielding brooms and yelling.

Caught in a deep sleep, Ami took too long to shake off her dopiness and run. She screamed when she felt the heavy blow of the wooden broom hit her ribs. The stunned Saluki sprinted after her friends as she dodged more strikes.

Layla raced away in the lead, checking every five strides to make sure her pack stayed close. They ran at full pelt - past their compound and the next - to the crossroads they all knew so well. Layla stopped and waited for the others to catch up. Brodie was the first to get there, followed by Mia, the little greyhound. Ami arrived last - the whack of the broom winded her, and she struggled to get her breath back.

Layla heard the Saluki's yelp of pain earlier, and she asked, "Are you okay?"

"Yeah, I'm fine," Ami spluttered, although her ribs throbbed as she wheezed and coughed. She'd never been one to make a fuss.

In familiar territory, the four hounds looked in the direction of their favourite spot to run - the place Lilian took them every day. They longed to be back there with her - darting among the mangroves, chasing birds, and sprinting along the beach in the warm shallow water.

"There won't be any water we can drink there." Layla cut the silence with the necessary, but unwelcome truth.

"We can just go for a bit. Please? Just a short while," Brodie pleaded.

"And when you make yourself really thirsty? What then?" Layla wasn't in the mood to entertain silly ideas. But, like the others, she yearned for some time out of their situation.

Morale broken, the pack fell silent again.

"We've got to go that way." Layla pointed her long nose straight ahead to a small town.

"But we don't know that place." Mia looked worried. She never liked to go anywhere without Lilian as it was, but venturing somewhere unknown without her human mother was a whole other level of terrifying.

Irritated by the comment, Layla grumbled, "I know, Mia. Do come up with a better suggestion, won't you?" As a reluctant leader, Layla's sensitivity to criticism seemed justified.

Abashed, Mia looked to the ground.

"Well, if we've got to go, then let's go!" Brodie declared, his attitude about their predicament less dogged than the others. He took the lead and sprang off toward the town.

"Watch out for dogs!" Layla called to the eager three-legged Azawakh that charged ahead.

"Right-o!" he cheerily called back, happy to lead the way. It satisfied his desire to protect his pack, a trait that came naturally to his breed.

As Brodie reached the first street, his eyes spotted something that made him stop dead – along the wall in front of him, a pipe steadily dripped. He gave it a sniff, then gleefully started to lick at the trickle of droplets. Etiquette flew out the window when the others caught up and pushed their heads in to drink.

Suddenly, Layla stopped and pulled her head out. The others didn't seem to notice or care as they continued to relish every precious drop.

"Guys," Layla spoke softly. "Guys," she raised her voice a little, given the previous lack of response. "Guys, stop!"

Brodie finally stopped to look at his leader, his gaze followed hers, and the lanky Azawakh froze.

"Guys, stop. Look!" Brodie's command worked, and Ami and Mia both looked up. Their gazes pivoted toward the lone dog that watched them with teeth bared.

Squaring up, Layla responded in kind, ready to fight.

"No, Layla," warned Ami as she took stock of the situation.

"I can take him," Layla slowly and calmly replied, her entire focus on the dog ahead of them. The resolute Sloughi made a step forward, but two more dogs appeared and flanked their leader as she did so. More mongrels appeared two-by-two until one dog became a ten-strong pack.

Layla stepped back.

"Move away, slowly. This is their water," cautioned Ami.

Led by Ami, the four thirsty intruders backed away from the pipe in absolute silence.

Layla observed the other pack until there was enough distance between them that the lead dog relaxed his aggressive stance.

"Let's go." Totally defeated, Layla realised that they would be powerless against other packs. *I can fight, and Ami isn't too bad, but Brodie will struggle,* she thought as they retreated. *He's already missing a front leg, and only one of his back legs is sturdy,* Layla reflected. *And Mia? She would probably be an excellent fighter if she were twenty kilos heavier,* the disgruntled leader silently mused.

Overwhelmed by despair, the harsh reality of their situation weighed on Layla. The others seemed to understand that things were serious, but not to the same degree. It's why Lilian called Layla her "thinker" - she saw things differently from the other dogs.

"Let's go to the beach," the black dog called back to her friends.

Three surprised faces looked Layla's way, and they all sped up.

* * * * *

It was a long run on a dusty road to get to the beach, and by the time they arrived, the hounds were exhausted. They ignored their fatigue and their thirst and ran straight into the water.

For a few moments, they experienced joy - carefree frolicking and splashing, the smells, birds to chase, and the warm water on their legs. Ami and Layla played tag on the sprawling beach, while Brodie and Mia snuffled through the remnants of old campfires.

When it was time to rest, the dogs all collapsed in a shady spot amongst the mangroves where they could look out across the ocean. They panted heavily and looked at each other with smiling eyes. In that moment, they felt pure elation.

But their happiness was short-lived. Although the pack thoroughly enjoyed the momentary escape, the day's events took a toll, and reality returned with a vengeance.

Brodie looked over to where Lilian usually parked her car. "I wish she was here."

The others nodded. Drained after their frenetic capers, the bone-weary pack reflected on the emptiness, the strangeness of their playtime without Lilian.

"I miss the way she chatted to us." Mia sobbed. "She was always talking to us, remember? Always. They both did."

Ami moved closer to the little grey dog, trying to comfort her.

"I miss the rubs," Brodie contributed to the sullen conversation. "Lilian always rubbed me after walks to stop my body hurting." Brodie looked down at his lone front leg, thinking about how sore his shoulder would be tomorrow.

"I miss the belly rubs," Ami sighed. Although they were less functional than Brodie's physiotherapy massage, Ami still got rubs every day, without fail.

Gazing into the distance, Layla kept silent. Of the four, she was the most bonded to Lilian. The pack leader hadn't shown any emotion about the situation previously, but, at that moment, Layla struggled to maintain her composure. "I just miss her," she quietly confessed.

Silence fell once more on the reflective foursome. Darkness soon followed suit. They were thirsty and hungry, but all they could do was find a safe place to sleep. Layla led the pack to the large sand mounds that they used to run up and down. They would be able to stay out of view and out of the wind if it picked up during the night. Brodie was the first to curl up, followed by Ami. Layla laid down next to the pair, and all three looked at the little greyhound who stood a few feet away and stared in horror.

"I can't sleep like this. I can't sleep... *here*," Mia whispered in consternation.

Layla rolled her eyes as she looked away.

"Mia, we don't have a choice." Ami gently admonished. Even hungry, thirsty, and exhausted, the motherly Saluki managed to be delicate.

"I can't sleep here. Let's go back home," Mia repeated.

"It's not home anymore, Mia. You know that." Ami tried to reason with her highly-strung packmate. "We'll find somewhere better tomorrow. It's too late to go wandering now."

Mia huffed as loudly as she could and curled up in the spot where she stood, refusing to join the others.

Brodie snored away, unaware of the drama.

"What was that?" Ami gasped.

"Wh...?" Layla looked at Ami, puzzled. Ami winked at her. "Oh! Oh yes, I definitely heard something," Layla joined in with the ruse.

"What? What did you hear?" Mia asked them as she cowered.

"Oh, it's stopped now. I hope it wasn't anything dangerous," Ami muttered as she put her head back down on the ground. A few seconds later, she felt a little warm body curled up behind her. Content, Ami smiled and fell fast asleep.

* * * * *

Layla was the first awake. She looked at the others and decided to let them sleep. Slumber offered their only escape from reality, and Layla didn't want to rouse her friends to the harsh light of day any sooner than necessary.

Dejectedly, Layla climbed the mound they slept next to and faced the early morning sun. She closed her eyes to ward off the sorrow - the previous day's conversation about Lilian and Tom hit her hard. Despite the heartache it caused, Layla reminisced about her first days with her human parents.

Layla's Story

Layla's neck throbbed. The dog watched in horror as her companions wailed and struggled. She shouted at them, "Keep moving, keep thrashing, keep shaking!" Her tortured calls accomplished nothing, and Layla watched the car drive off at speed as it dragged the two doomed dogs behind it. The shaken Sloughi would never forget their screams.

Injuries caused by Layla's desperate escape from the brutal treatment were fresh and made her choke when she swallowed. She was desperately hungry – there hadn't been any food for many weeks.

The battered dog was thirsty. Layla couldn't recall the last time she had more than a few licks of water. The ruthless handlers kept her just alive enough to entertain them.

She wandered the area but didn't go too far in case the savage men came back with the other dogs. *Maybe they could still escape,* Layla worriedly pondered. That thought gave Layla pause, and she decided to wait for them.

Wearily, she found a quiet spot and tucked herself away. Layla cowered as she curled up her battered body – a wincing, shivering, throbbing mass of pain. The cold night air seeped into her bruised frame. Without her family to bundle up with, it took Layla a long time to fall asleep. And once she did, vivid nightmares replayed her torment, so it was not an easy slumber.

The sun gently woke Layla; its warmth welcomed on her chilled, beaten body. She laid there for some time, contemplating her next steps. She desperately needed water, so Layla pulled herself to her feet. Abused muscles screamed in protest as she did. Slowly, Layla paced around the area, looking for anything that might contain water from the last rainstorm. She suppressed the feeling of despair that grew deep in her stomach as she moved from one area to another, finding nothing but dust and rubbish.

"Hey!"

A person stood across from her, and Layla froze.

"Hey, yalla." The stranger gestured to a bowl on the ground.

Layla's thirst, along with her curiosity, dictated her actions, and she slowly walked over to the lone man. When she got within ten feet of him, he backed away and pointed at the bowl full of water on the ground. Layla lowered her head to take a few licks, keeping her eyes fixed on the provider.

Her throat ached, but she was too thirsty to care. The Sloughi lifted her head and looked harder at the stranger. He took a few more steps back, and Layla lowered her head again, drinking as quickly as she could. With every sip, the abused animal felt more and more grateful to the newcomer who gave what she so desperately needed.

With her thirst sated, Layla looked up and moved closer to the man. She stopped a few feet in front of him when he pointed something at her - a small rectangular item. It clicked a few times, and with that, the man left and went into a house.

Layla followed him but stopped short of the gate. The dog's distrustful nature resumed command with her thirst quenched, and she returned to her hiding spot. She needed recovery time to heal her battered body.

Dusk tinged the sky when Layla got up again. The rest did her good, but she was painfully hungry, so the emaciated animal decided to scavenge. Safer in the shadows as darkness fell, Layla wandered the area with her nose to the ground, but the search yielded nothing. Not one scrap, not one morsel.

She looked up and saw the kind stranger's house, so she walked closer to the gate and looked through. If the man helped her once, maybe he'd do it again. Convinced, Layla sat down and decided to wait.

It was some time before she heard the door open, and the same man walked to the gate. He threw out two slices of pizza, and Layla ran to collect them. Usually, she'd eat one and save the other, but her hunger was far too great, and she chomped through them both quickly. The ravenous dog looked up at the man who stood behind the gate, and he threw a third slice behind her. She ran to get it, and he opened the gate, placing another bowl of water on the ground before closing it and going back into the house. Layla finished the meal in a few bites and ran over to the water bowl. She drank without restraint until her tummy swelled.

Content, Layla laid down by the water bowl and felt a brief moment of peace.

However, the quiet didn't last. Layla jumped to her feet as she heard an all-too-familiar noise. Screeching tyres and revving engines sent fear coursing through her tense body, and Layla braced herself.

Lights flashed in her eyes, and she frantically searched for somewhere to hide. Layla darted behind a large bin as three cars pulled up to the same spot as before. She watched as one of them opened a window and threw something large out of the vehicle before they sped off again.

Silence reigned once more as Layla tried to make out what the man threw from the car. The curious dog approached, and as she did, the object moved. Layla caught it's scent, and her slow, cautious walk turned into a full sprint.

"Mother!" Layla called as she approached the injured animal that dragged herself out of the way to a nearby wall.

Layla couldn't conceal her shock. "Mum, it's me."

Aaliyah shifted her head a fraction so she could see the black dog that towered over her. The tortured matriarch used the last of her energy to move to safety before she said, "Layla. My child... you're... alive." Aaliyah struggled to get the words out of her swollen throat.

"Yes, I'm here. I'm here with you now." Layla licked the blood off her mother's wounds, but the action amplified her mother's pain as the brutalized dog groaned and pawed at the dirt.

"Stop, Layla... it's no good... no good." Aaliyah knew the agony would fade, and she would be at peace soon.

"Asim?" Layla's voice quivered as she asked about her brother. Aaliyah's eyes provided Layla with her answer. Grieved, Layla threw her head up and wailed with the pain of it all, only to be stopped by a paw gently touching hers. She looked at the broken body of her dying mother and laid down, curling up protectively around her.

"You have to leave this place, my daughter. You have... to be strong... and brave." Aaliyah summoned the last of her strength to get her final words out. "Remember... how fast you are. Remember... to always be... cautious."

Layla nodded, absorbing her mother's instruction.

"Remember... that I love you."

Gently, Layla licked her mother's mouth as she watched the mangled matriarch take her last laboured breath.

Hours passed, and Layla didn't move a muscle. She stayed, curled up with her mother, unwilling to leave her side, but Layla knew she needed to go. Cars moved in and out of the area, but Layla stayed concealed by a tree. It wouldn't be long until someone noticed her.

Layla's stomach rumbled. Her hunger was back, and she wanted to seek out the kind man in the hope that he would give her more food.

Mournfully, Layla lifted her head and looked at her mother's face. After a last, gentle lick on her nose, Layla walked away with a shattered heart.

She got to the fence and found two cars parked outside the kind man's house. The vehicles obscured the gate, so she wasn't visible to those inside. Layla waited by the cars for some time, pacing back and forth but staying in the area. Suddenly she heard voices and bolted behind one of the vehicles.

They were female voices, and they seemed to be getting louder. "Come on; it's okay."

Layla peered around the car to see two women looking straight at her.

"It's okay. Come on, come here!" one softly called.

The females crouched and threw pieces of food in Layla's direction. She sniffed a morsel close to her and swallowed it down quickly. There was another piece just in reach, so she slowly crept out and got that one too.

The ladies' voices were soft and kind, not like the harsh shouts of the violent people that tied her to the car. An unfamiliar sense of safety comforted Layla, so she decided to get closer to them and the bowl of food they placed on the ground.

"That's it; it's okay. We won't hurt you."

Layla stopped in front of the women, startled when one of them touched the top of her head. Nervously, Layla dropped away from the hand, but the lady reached further and touched Layla's shoulders.

Devastated by the weight of her circumstances and loss, Layla felt heavier than ever. Vanquished, the poor animal lowered her guard and allowed the attention.

The woman gently stroked Layla and continued to speak quietly, comforting the skittish hound until she ultimately submitted. "You poor thing," the lady consoled as the other opened one of the cars.

Alarm flooded Layla's system, but her world-weary spirit gave up the battle. She didn't even fight the collar secured around her neck. Once lifted and placed inside the car, the terrified dog immediately began to salivate and shake with fear.

Then the doors closed and the vehicle started to move! Overwhelmed with dread, Layla drooled and trembled for the entire journey. When the car stopped, the shaken Sloughi held her breath.

What is going to happen? How can I escape? she wondered in dismay.

The car door opened, and the woman attached a leash to the makeshift collar Layla wore. She obediently followed the lady, who took her to a small shed-like room. Panic set in when the woman left Layla there and closed the door. Terrified, the Sloughi cowered in the corner, looking around for some way out. *Did I make a mistake trusting these women?* she despaired.

Before Layla could gather her thoughts, the lady returned with a large crate, which she placed in the middle of the room. The rescuer pulled out a soft blanket, arranged it inside, and then gently led the timid animal to the bed. Layla saw the comfortable space and immediately crawled inside.

The tired dog curled up as the lady stroked Layla and spoke to her: "You're safe now, sweetheart."

The next morning, Layla woke to the sound of a door and waited for someone to appear by her crate. But the first thing she saw was a massive plate of food. Cautiously, Layla snuck bite after bite while the lady spoke to her, and the traumatized pup relaxed. The lurking dread eased. After Layla ate all her upset stomach could handle, the woman secured the leash and led her out of the room.

Layla's new friend took her to a patch of grass and walked the grateful animal up and down. After another cold night, Layla took advantage of the sun's warm rays and laid down. The lady sat with her for a while before she returned Layla to the crate.

For the next five days, the animal and the woman established a routine. Layla's caretaker provided food and water three times a day, and after the dog ate, they'd wander outside for a walk. But as each day passed, Layla's discontent grew. The young Sloughi liked the safety of the crate, but she hated being trapped in the dark room – unable to flee if needed. Layla missed her freedom.

Late on the sixth night, Layla woke to the sound of human voices. She lifted her head and strained to listen. Only one of the voices seemed familiar. When the door opened, Layla spotted the lady she knew and two other people - one man and one woman. Immediately the trio crouched by the crate, and Layla gazed back at the faces. The unfamiliar female spoke to the hesitant animal - her voice gentle, her face kind - and Layla immediately felt drawn to her. Comfortable in the woman's presence, Layla emerged from the crate, and as soon as she did, the lady stroked a hand over the Sloughi's black coat. Layla relaxed – calmed by a sense of serenity.

"Hello sweetie... hello Layla," the new lady exclaimed as she led Layla out of the room. The young hound appreciated the woman's excitement, and it made her feel even more comfortable. Layla fed off the positive energy and jumped up at the happy woman. The energetic female smiled warmly and let Layla stretch up to smell her face.

Pleased, the lady looked up at the tall man, who smiled just as warmly and reached out to stroke Layla on the neck.

"Okay, we better get going," he said as he led Layla to a car. The tall man opened the door, and the new woman got in and arranged some blankets beside her. He handed the leash to the lady and looked expectantly at Layla. After a few seconds, he reached down to pick her up, and Layla let him.

The dog felt nervous but not fearful like the first time she rode in a car. Layla laid down next to the new woman, and they drove away. However, Layla started to drool, and she couldn't seem to stop.

Layla soon learned the woman was called Lilian. In an effort to comfort the dog, the lady kept a hand on Layla for the whole journey. Lilian talked to her throughout the ride. When the car stopped, Lilian got out and walked around the vehicle to Layla's side. The hound froze when the door opened, so Lilian lifted her out.

"She's so light," Lilian exclaimed to her husband, Tom.

"I know, there's nothing to her," he replied.

Once inside, Layla looked around for a place to hide. She made for the dining room table and crawled in-between the legs of the chairs.

"Just let her be for a bit," she heard Lilian say.

As the couple went about their business, Layla watched and gradually discovered she didn't need to fear the kind people. Fighting her cautious streak was tricky, but Layla really wanted to go to them.

And once she spotted Tom sprawled out on the carpet, Layla couldn't help herself. As a young dog, the temptation to romp about proved to be too much: she bound out from under the table and nudged him to play. It had been so long since the Sloughi allowed herself to be silly and carefree.

Lilian giggled from her spot on the floor as she watched Layla frolic and run in small circles. After a short while, Lilian beckoned Layla toward a bed under the stairs. The new doggy mommy quickly figured out that Layla refused to climb them, so Lillian brought her bed downstairs instead.

Layla wiggled with happiness - she'd never felt such softness before! Lilian and Tom stayed with her for a while - stroking, talking, and smiling at her - before they went upstairs to bed.

Suddenly alone, Layla felt uneasy, but it wasn't enough to keep her awake, and she fell into a deep sleep.

Layla awoke disoriented, and it took a few minutes to remember where she was. Scared by the quietness of the home, Layla didn't want to move or make noise. Tucked away under the stairs, Layla stayed in her bed until she heard footsteps. Then two smiling faces peered in at her.

"Hello, angel. Are you awake now? You want some breakfast?" Lilian asked as she and Tom slowly approached the dog's bed.

Trembling, Layla crept halfway out to greet them - she didn't want to leave the safety of her nest. And Lilian could see that, so she brought Layla's food to her.

Lilian sat with Layla at each meal, and that's how it went for the next three days. Layla slept and ate, then slept and ate more.

Layla quickly became very fond of her human mother. Lilian was with Layla - sitting beside her, reading to her, or just talking to her - constantly.

On the evening of Layla's third day, things seemed to change. Lilian's energy altered completely: she cried all the time and stopped talking. The lady stayed upstairs and did not come down for very long periods, and Layla didn't understand what happened. Confused, Layla mused, *What is wrong with her? Is she injured?*

Two days passed, and there was no change in Lilian. Layla was still not at ease roaming the house, save for dashing outside to pee, but she found herself missing her new friend.

Layla saw Tom, and he would give her food and sit with her, but it felt strange without Lilian.

On the third day, a worried Layla decided to find her. Although the prospect made her shake with trepidation, the dog knew she had to climb the stairs. So, she took a deep breath and climbed, step-after-step, pausing to listen with every move. Layla wondered if she'd be able to get down them again when she got to the top and looked around.

There were five rooms upstairs, doors all ajar. Testing the air, Layla threw her nose up then headed to the closest room on her left. She stopped when she was just inside the door and looked at the bed. Facing away from her, Lilian laid all curled up, and Layla could sense her melancholy. It was overwhelmingly familiar.

Layla wanted to be with Lilian the same way Lilian had been with her the past few days. When Layla jumped onto the bed and stood over her companion, Lilian turned and looked at the dog through swollen eyes. The woman smiled, turned around to face the curious hound, and put a hand out to stroke her. It relieved Layla to feel Lilian's gentle touch again, and she laid down beside her.

Lilian curled her body around Layla's and sobbed quietly. Layla knew she had fallen asleep when the hand Lilian used to stroke her stopped and rested heavily on Layla's shoulder. Once the nerves of being up on the bed subsided, Layla fell into a deep slumber as well.

There were many more days before Lilian returned to her usual self, and the two stayed hip to hip through it all. As time passed, Layla became more comfortable in the home Lilian and Tom shared with her.

They went for long walks together, she got more food than she could eat, Layla never had to search for water, and the content hound slept wherever she chose.

Lilian and Tom never tied her up, shouted, pushed, or kicked her – they showed her love. Layla didn't know how she ended up there, but she never wanted to leave.

It was a good hour before the others woke. Bright sunlight broke over the crest of the mound that shaded them.

Layla's trip down memory lane left her with a melancholy that was hard to shake.

Brodie stretched and ran back to the beach while Mia pranced behind him.

Ami climbed the mound to sit beside Layla. "We need to find water," the Saluki announced.

Layla nodded.

"Food would be good, too," Ami added.

Layla looked up to the sky and down again. "Do you remember that time you and I went all the way up there?" Layla motioned to the long dirt road to their left.

"Yes, and I remember how upset Lilian was when we came back."

They smiled at the memory. Whenever the dogs went off alone, they found Lilian's worried reactions funny. Their smiles soon weakened.

"She really loved us, didn't she?" Ami looked over to their pack mates as the pair frolicked. Layla's sigh was her answer.

"So, what about that place? You think we should go?" Ami continued. "There were a few houses there. I think it's worth a try. There's nothing here but saltwater."

Layla nodded in agreement, and Ami went to collect the others.

It was a short run to their destination, but Mia and Brodie already tired themselves out with playtime. And the prospect that there might not be water available made them hang their heads, so Layla told everyone to take it slowly.

The journey made Layla sadder with every step. It was all so familiar.

Once, the place brought such comfort to her. She eyed the jagged ridges of the hard sand mounds – places she'd run with Lilian. A few weeks earlier, part of the ridge gave way under Lilian's foot. She'd tumbled down the face, and Layla recalled the taste of blood licked from Lilian's injured knees.

The dirt road ended and opened into a large clearing with two houses straight ahead and two more on the right. Mia pointed her nose in the air and sniffed hard. "You smell that?" she asked the others.

"Yes, I smell it," Layla replied, her face hardening. They could all smell it. There were other dogs in the area.

"Maybe they've left?" Brodie asked hopefully.

"Let's stay together. Stay close," the pack leader commanded as she walked cautiously toward the first home. Carefully, the others followed Layla in complete silence.

The black dog stopped, tipped her head toward the clearing, and gestured to the Azawakh. Brodie nodded to show Layla he understood the directions and slowly dropped behind to watch their backs.

The gate to the house's garden was open, so Layla pushed her head in to look around. It was clear, and there weren't any bends or corners that other dogs could lurk behind.

Layla spotted a large trough that glistened brightly in the sun. "Water!" the hound exclaimed as she ran over. The others followed as Layla instructed.

The leader dipped her tongue. "It's good!"

The trough was so large that they could all drink at the same time. The relief the pack felt made them giddy, and they giggled as they drank.

"As much as you can!" Ami told them. "Fill your bellies!" Elated, the Saluki celebrated the long drink, knowing it would take the edge off her hunger pangs.

When they were all done, they trotted to the open area outside the house to lie down, their bellies sloshing as they went. "What a find!" exclaimed Ami. She shot a smile at the others and got three grins back in return.

* * * * *

"I'm so hungry." Brodie was the first to say.

"Me too!" Mia added.

"Layla, we've got to find some food. We're starving." Ami looked at her friend, who was deep in thought.

The Sloughi took time to respond. "I have to hunt," Layla solemnly acknowledged.

No one said anything. Layla hadn't hunted in many years, and she didn't even know if she could anymore. The mice that lived under the stairs were the only animals Layla managed to catch since Lilian adopted her.

The others looked around the barren landscape, searching for a better solution to their hunger problem.

"It's so dead here," Brodie uttered as he looked for some life in the distance.

"I'll wait until the sun sets," Layla replied.

At dusk, the seabirds rested for the night, and the desert hares came out of their burrows.

"I'll go with you," Ami quietly told Layla, who responded with a look of disbelief. Ami hung her head. The Saluki's penchant for food and dislike of exercise led to weight gain over the years, and Ami knew she'd be no help.

Brodie enthusiastically shouted, "I'll go!"

Ami shot Layla the usual look that told the reluctant leader to be kind in her response to the eager tri-paw.

"Who will protect Ami and Mia when I'm gone, though? You need to be here in case anything bad happens," was Layla's uncharacteristically thoughtful response.

It wasn't that Brodie wasn't fast; he was swift. The disabled Azawakh learned to alter his gallop to accommodate his weak back leg, and he could really shift. It was Layla and Ami's protective instincts that encouraged him to stay put.

From the moment Lilian brought the injured dog home, she kept him wrapped in cotton wool. The other hounds saw how worried Lillian became over the long months of his extended recovery. And the pack recognized Lilian's concern – she squinted her eyes and drew a short, sharp breath every time Brodie descended the face of a sand mound. In her absence, they echoed Lillian's protective nature.

Brodie looked disappointed, but when he saw Ami's worried face, he puffed out his chest and stood as tall as possible. "Okay, I'll hold the fort here then."

* * * * *

Layla took a few licks of water. She wanted to fill her belly again, but the hound knew it would limit her speed if she did. With a few hours left before sunset, Layla felt the weight of the world on her shoulders. Layla tensed when she realised her pack depended on her to return with food.

Without any apparent sign of her nervousness, Layla bid the others a brisk farewell and headed off.

"Good luck!" the Saluki cheered.

"You can do it!" Brodie enthused.

Layla stopped for a moment and then carried on without looking back. The encouragement from her pack members was not appreciated.

"I've never ever been this hungry," Mia complained. "I think I'm going to die," the little greyhound dramatically moaned.

Ami gave Mia a sideways look but didn't say anything. Deep in thought, Ami frowned. She *had* been this hungry before, and the ache brought back painful memories Ami had tried to bury.

Ami's Story

Ami strained as her belly heaved. This was harder than it had been before - she was exhausted and panting. The three puppies she already delivered mewed and wriggled against her chest. The proud mother licked them as they felt their way towards her teats.

Ami pulled her head up and panted harder. She needed to catch her breath before she tried to birth the last of her litter. The weary Saluki strained again as a contraction started, and with one final push, Ami delivered.

Immediately, Ami knew something was wrong. The silent pup didn't move, so Ami licked him vigorously. He didn't respond. The frantic mother licked the tiny wet body harder and harder until a hand got in her way. She watched as the man inspected the lifeless body. He rubbed her puppy in his hands then looked at him for a while.

"Wait!" cried Ami as she watched the human leave the barn with her lifeless child. Her eyes fixed on the door, waiting for him to come back. When he did return, her puppy was nowhere to be seen.

As her remaining three puppies suckled, the brokenhearted hound whined and whined, but there was no reaction from the man standing over her. The human reached for the babies, and Ami froze in fear. *Not again,* she thought to herself. *Please, don't take them again.*

One by one, he picked up each pup, turned them over, and looked into their faces. Ami was relieved when he returned them all to her, then he left and closed the door behind him.

Ami's eyes fixed on the entrance once again as she patiently waited for him to return with her lost puppy. Hours passed, but no one came. Ami couldn't stay awake - the long and difficult birth took every last ounce of her energy - her head lowered, and the mother fell asleep.

Early the next morning, Ami woke to the squeak of the door. She looked up, bleary-eyed but hopeful. *Does he have my son?* she worried. Ami deflated - all the man carried was a bowl of food. Though saddened, the new mother was also ravenous and didn't hesitate to eat.

Weeks went by in the same fashion until Ami accepted that her son was gone. Instead, she focused her love and attention on the three growing babies, whose personalities started to shine through.

Ami adored her lovely children, but the tense mother couldn't shake the dread of what was in store. As Ami's fourth litter, she knew exactly what was ahead for her puppies.

* * * * *

Ami winced. It was a familiar cry, but she never got used to it. She gazed across the room, where her son wailed. He called desperately for her, but there was nothing she could do.

Ami whimpered as the man sliced into one tiny ear and then the other while her baby boy writhed and screamed. Sickened, Ami watched the bloody pieces of severed flesh fall to the floor. The man dropped her son, who immediately ran back to his mother. Ami licked at the bloody stubs and wept, knowing the puppy would not be with her much longer.

The Saluki lived through this horror over and over: Ami only got a few months with her family before they were taken away. She looked at her crying, shaking puppy and felt the same helplessness she'd felt with her other children. Ami was powerless to protect them: her son would be taken, put into a training program, and the whole cycle would begin again.

The melancholic mother took a long look at her son and sniffed him – she never wanted to forget his smell. Her boy screamed for Ami as he was picked up and taken away for the last time, never to feel his mother's touch again.

Ami's heart shattered as she curled up with her two daughters and pulled them in close. She had more time with them, but Ami knew what their fate would be - they would be subjected to the same sorrow-filled life Ami lived for two years. Her daughters would have family after family ripped from them and then exist in perpetual despair and misery.

Three months went by while Ami attempted to enjoy what little time she had left with the two puppies that remained. The dogs were permitted to roam the farm, but not the training area.

Every so often, in the distance, Ami caught a glimpse of her son as he worked. The pup looked strong and fast. She hoped with all her heart that he was, because Ami knew what happened to the dogs who didn't win.

Soon, Ami would be separated from her daughters, and she tried to suppress the panic. She didn't want to worry them, so Ami spent every moment with them - playing, sleeping, and grooming. They were oblivious to what their futures would hold.

Early one morning, Ami woke when two men approached. They walked with determination and wore hard, mean expressions. They clipped a leash onto her collar, and Ami got a little excited - she hadn't gone for a run in so long. Before her first litter, the breeders took her out for regular exercise, so Ami trotted after them as they led her out of the compound.

Still dopey from the early wake-up call, her two daughters were picked up and brought along. Loaded into a car that sped away so fast it caused Ami to lose her footing, the dog's moment of excitement rapidly disappeared. Something felt very wrong. Ami softly whined as she watched the scenery flash past.

"Shhhh!"

Ami yelped and jumped back when one of the men smacked her on the nose.

"Here," one of the men said. The strangers pulled off the road and got out. They threw open the door, grabbed Ami's leash, and yanked the frightened dog out of the car, along with her daughters. The harsh men roughly pulled her collar off, got back into the car, and drove away.

Bewildered, Ami watched until it was out of sight. She looked around, not recognising anything about the area. The reality of her situation slowly dawned on her.

"Where are we?" asked the pups in unison.

"I don't know. I've never been here before."

The trio took shelter from the sun under some wooden boards propped up against a mound of dirt at an abandoned construction site.

While her daughters laid down and fell back to sleep, Ami slowly walked around the area. A desolate waste ground surrounded them – no cars, no people, no animals.

With dread, Ami realised they'd been cast out. *We're on our own,* she silently despaired. And it took all of Ami's concentration to hide her panic from the puppies.

"Mumma, we're hungry," Ami's tiniest daughter said as she stretched awake.

The puppies hadn't a clue how serious the situation was - they were still in "eat, sleep, play" mode. Ami knew their plea for food was coming, and she was hungry too. She never needed to find food before - it had always been provided.

Pensively, Ami cast her mind back to when she found a wrapper full of chicken bones near a bin in their compound. She'd remembered because Ami could see a bin dead ahead in the distance. Maybe she'd find food there.

Ami paused, her hesitation caused by indecision about whether to bring her puppies along. She wanted to go alone, but would they really stay hidden if she did? The uncertain mother decided to take the chance. "I'm going to look for something for us to eat. It's very important that you stay here. Stay hidden. Do not come after me. I won't be long. Okay?"

The two little girls looked up at their mother and nodded in unison. The prospect of food made good behaviour more likely, although it certainly wasn't guaranteed.

Ami quickly headed toward the bin. Sniffing voraciously, she pawed through the overflow of rubbish in search of anything that smelled like food. Bingo! Ami discovered a bag full of vegetable skins and peels. With the bag hanging from her jaws, the Saluki victoriously returned to her concealed children. The puppies patiently waited until Ami dropped the bounty, then they dived into the bag.

"I don't like this," said her firstborn, as she chewed on a potato skin with a scowl.

"It's all we have for now. It'll stop you feeling hungry," was the mother's gentle response. Ami waited for her pups to have their fill, and then she finished what little was left. They all curled up and slept some more.

Although the morning took its toll on Ami, it took a while for the tired hound to fall asleep - kept awake by the all-consuming worry of fending for her family.

* * * * *

After a troubled sleep, Ami slowly opened her eyes. She lifted her head, looked around, and found she was alone. The fearful parent jumped up as if jabbed with a cattle prod. Frantic, Ami constantly called for her daughters. She ran zigzags around the area, but there was no sign or sound of them.

Ami's wide eyes scanned the distance as she panted in panic, then she heard something. She turned to one side and tilted her head to hear better. *Was that... laughter?*

Following the sound, Ami jogged past a housing compound to a parallel road. And there were her two naughty children - playing and giggling as they darted in and out of the sprinklers.

Ami breathed an almighty sigh and bolted toward them. The frolicking pups froze, bracing themselves for a serious telling off when they saw Ami approaching. Instead, their very relieved mum covered the pair with a barrage of kisses. "Well, I guess we know where to find water! Well done, you two!"

The ditzy puppies did not realise what their amusing find meant for their survival.

Ami found a collection of the run-off water and drank as much as she could fit in her belly. Thirst quenched, she looked at her puppies as sternly as her kind face allowed. "You must never, ever leave my side again, do you understand? This is a dangerous place. You have to stay with me, okay?"

The puppies nodded in unison.

"Come on, back to our spot," the relieved mother directed.

The inevitable questions began as they made their way back to their safe space. "Why have they left us here?" asked one pup.

"When are they going to come back, Mumma?" said the other.

Ami hesitated to answer. What response could she give that wouldn't worry the pair?

9

When dusk fell, their bellies grumbled once again. Looking at the complaining puppies, Ami continued to fret. She didn't want to leave them but knew she had no other choice. Firmly, the mother dog told them to stay exactly where they were and trotted off, blindly hoping they would obey this time.

Ami headed to the bin she visited previously. There was nothing there, so she moved further down the road until she came to an intersection.

She caught a promising scent, so Ami followed it to the left. The fantastic smell got stronger, and Ami quickened her pace. The unbearable ache in her empty belly overshadowed Ami's caution as she ran straight past three shadowy figures.

They pulled out and started to chase the intruder.

Ami caught a glimpse behind her and realised she was being followed. She stopped and turned to look at the animals. Facing her, they halted when she did and stood lined up, side by side. Three more of the pack appeared a little way behind her. Ami turned, then turned again. She wagged her tail and bent her head down to show she did not pose a threat.

Slowly, Ami walked to her right, hoping to slink away. But as she moved, so did the pack – every move in tandem - she stopped, they stopped. She moved to her left, and so did they, taunting her.

Silently, Ami took a deep breath and looked around for a gap. Could she outrun them? She hadn't really run for years!

Ami hung her head further, in the hope of placating the waiting pack. Suddenly, a seventh dog appeared in front of Ami, approaching with less hostility. By the pack's reaction to him, Ami assumed he was the leader, and she looked at him with huge, frightened eyes.

The Alpha studied her composure, then looked around at his pack. They withdrew immediately, and he moved out of her way. Ami kept her head low as she slowly walked out of the area. The frightened Saluki didn't look behind her; she simply walked until she was out of their sight.

Overwhelmed, Ami collapsed in the dirt and caught her breath. "That was too close!" she whimpered. They could have killed her if they wanted to, and what would become of her puppies if she couldn't get back to them?

Unwilling to take any more chances that night, the hungry dog returned to find her daughters fast asleep - blissfully unaware of their dire situation.

* * * * *

"Mumma, I'm so hungry."

Ami woke as her puppies whined and pawed at her belly. "There's no more, my children." How she wished she still had milk to feed them! "Let's go and get water. That will help fill your tummies."

They headed back to the sprinklers. It wouldn't be enough to keep them going for long. They were all starving, and Ami didn't know what to do.

"Can't we go back, Mumma? Back home?"

Ami looked at her child. "I don't know where home is, and I don't think they want us there anymore."

She hadn't wanted to worry them, but she was running out of indirect answers to their questions. "It's just us now. We have to find a way to live out here."

Ami watched as the two puppies digested the information. They didn't ask any more questions. They just moved closer to their mother as if to comfort her. Ami realised her worry must show more than she knew. "I've got to go and look for food again. You two stay hidden, okay? Don't go wandering."

The bolder of the two puppies stood up. "Mumma, we'll come. We'll help."

Before the previous night's encounter, Ami might have taken them up on the offer, but she was too scared to risk it now. "No. You have to stay here. I won't be long. Stay hidden."

"But, Mumma!" protested the pup.

"Stay here." Ami was firm in her response, and her daughter reluctantly accepted it.

With that, Ami left. This time, her puppies laid down and watched her go – weak with hunger, they had no more energy left to play. It weighed heavy on her as she departed because Ami could see how much of their puppy fat had melted away already.

The memory of last night fresh in her mind, Ami trotted slowly to the crossroads and took the opposite street. She slowed to a walk, very well aware that there may be many more dogs in the area.

She approached a parade of shops and cautiously walked behind the buildings, avoiding the roadside. The thankful mother's eyes grew wide when she saw exactly what she needed - bin after bin lined up.

She looked around in utter disbelief. *Surely, I can't be the first to discover this place,* Ami mused. Once the dog was confident she was alone, she wasted no time.

Rifling through the bins systematically, the ecstatic Saluki discovered a bounty of food. There were packets of bread rolls, bags of discarded bones, and all kinds of vegetable off-cuts. Ami stretched her mouth wide and wedged in as much as she was able to, clamping down tight so she wouldn't drop a morsel.

Just as she turned, Ami felt an almighty whack on her backside. The stunned dog let out a muffled cry as she glanced behind her to see the angry face of the man that yelled at her. Terrified, Ami ran as fast as she could and soon arrived back at her camp.

She dropped the food as her two sleepy pups slowly opened their eyes. They quickly livened up when they realised what their mum brought them. Ami watched them tuck in as her daughters descended on the pile of food.

Knowing what she brought wouldn't last long, Ami needed to go back and get more. She took a few bites of a bread roll, told her pups to stay out of sight, and set off again.

Ami neared the parade of shops. The sting of the whack she received on the last trip still lingered along her spine. The nervous Saluki crept around cars and bins, staying out of the light wherever she could and darting through it wherever she couldn't. She carefully collected another bundle of food; eyes fixed on the doorway where the angry man dwelled.

Ami felt her energy wane, but she took off once more as fast as she could. The mother dog needed to get as much of the food to her puppies as possible, and the heat made food spoil so quickly. Soon it would rot, and Ami would need to find more elsewhere.

Ami made three more successful trips, and as a result, her puppies were asleep with swollen bellies and happy faces. Ami finally felt at ease. She'd done it - she filled their hungry tummies. Ami sat and watched the puppies sleep while she ate a little to keep her strength up.

Pensively, Ami looked around and wondered if she should risk one more trip. Worried about how long it might take to find more food, Ami got up and made her way toward the shops. There wasn't much left, but Ami took what she could find and set off more slowly this time. Her puppies were fed and would sleep for hours. She had eaten and felt better for it. There was no rush to get back, so instead of a brisk gallop, Ami trotted.

Too many easy trips made Ami drop her guard, and it took her a long time to notice the dark, shadowy figure that followed her. The mongrel watched every shop dash Ami made, but Ami didn't catch a glimpse of him until she made a sharp turn. As soon as she noticed him, the mongrel rushed her, and he was fast. Ami turned and bolted, but she wasn't quick enough to outrun him. Within seconds he was next to her, snapping and growling.

Ami yelped as she stumbled, then rolled over and over, the food flying from her jaws and scattering all over the ground. When she stopped reeling, Ami shook and tried to get her bearings. The large male dog paced malevolently, baring his teeth and staring at Ami with intense, angry eyes. Ami knew he could sense her fear.

She quickly glanced down at the scattered food. "Take it," the frightened Saluki murmured. Ami assumed that was what the fierce animal wanted. She slowly walked backward, trying to put as much distance between them as possible. Ami just wanted to get back to her pups. She watched as he slowly gathered the items, never breaking his gaze.

"And the rest?" he growled.

A cold chill shot down Ami's spine. "That's all of it," she replied in terror.

"I watched you make many trips. Where did you take it all?"

Ami had to think quickly. She couldn't take the mangy cur back to her camp and endanger her puppies. But, the stray's intense stare said that he wouldn't back down.

"Okay, I'll show you," Ami calmly replied as she led him in the opposite direction of her base. Careful not to arouse his suspicion, Ami thoughtfully considered her route. He'd observed her previous path, so the timid mother needed to convince the mongrel that was their destination.

As he trotted mere feet behind her, Ami racked her brains. She couldn't outrun him, and she couldn't fight him. Beyond that, Ami doubted her ability to outsmart him, but it seemed the only recourse.

"How much further? You didn't take so long before?" the mutt grumbled as he trailed further behind the anxious mother dog.

"Not much further. I normally run faster than this," Ami submissively replied.

She was a dog with above-ordinary endurance built into her breeding, and Ami noticed the large male lost more ground as they continued. Unequipped for long-distances, the scrappy mutt was built for short, fast bursts, and his fatigue showed.

Her pace steady, Ami knew precisely where to lead the tired hound as the stalker continued to drop back. Nervous about returning to the area that she barely got out of alive, Ami's brain scrambled for a better idea. Still, Ami slowed to a trot as she neared the street and scanned for signs of the hostile pack.

When Ami's pursuer caught up, the cur's mouth pulled back at the edges and revealed all of his teeth as he panted hard, and slobber poured off his tongue. Ami panted too, but she knew she had distance left in her.

"Well? Where's the food?" snapped her captor.

Ami could just make out a dark shape in the near distance where a perpendicular street began. "There, behind the bin," she replied, motioning ahead with her long nose.

Perhaps the run increased his hunger and clouded his judgement because the dog ran straight to where Ami motioned without caution. Ami stood stock still as she watched four startled dogs jump straight up and descend on the ignorant intruder. Then Ami turned and fled as fast as she could go, hearing his cries of pain as she escaped.

She ran hard and fast and didn't slow until she got back to her puppies. The grateful mother greeted her daughters warmly, relieved to be safely back with them.

As she finally put her head down to rest, Ami reflected on her actions. She didn't feel good about the deadly deception. But watching her two children play alleviated the guilt enough that Ami dropped off into a well-needed, deep sleep.

* * * * *

Four days after the food ran out, Ami's stomach hurt - but not as bad as her heart. After multiple unsuccessful trips to find more food, the starved puppies wasted away before Ami's eyes. The encounter with the aggressive dog made Ami terrified to venture too far from her family, but she knew that she was out of options.

It took all morning to summon the courage, but Ami resolved to go as far as necessary to find the food needed to keep her babies alive. Wistfully, she gazed at her daughters before Ami sighed and ventured off.

Her stomach hurt, her head hurt, and her body felt weak and wobbly. But Ami pushed through and managed to keep a steady pace. All of Ami's hope rested on one last route.

A person spotted Ami almost as soon as she arrived on the new street. The anxious dog stopped fast and prepared to turn heel and flee, but the person's demeanour made Ami hesitate.

The woman didn't shout angrily and flail her arms to shoo the Saluki away. Instead, the human crouched and called to Ami in a quiet, gentle voice. With an arm outstretched, the lady slowly moved toward Ami, talking like the dog's favourite caretaker on the farm.

Ami bowed her head and shuffled towards the kind stranger, looking up now and then to see if the woman's demeanour would change. It had been so long since she had been stroked or had a belly rub that Ami couldn't resist the woman's coos. And the moment she felt a gentle hand on her head, Ami melted inside.

Nervous but relieved to feel affection once again, Ami moved closer, and the woman rested both hands on the dog, speaking softly. The gentle stranger ran her hands over Ami's protruding ribs and bony hips. Then she cradled Ami's face in her hands and looked into the gentle mother dog's deep brown eyes.

When the woman stood up and beckoned for Ami to follow, the Saluki did so, without even thinking. Ami followed the kind woman into a garden and received a bounty of food and water. Ami's intense hunger made her wolf down the food in one go.

The lady went inside the house while Ami ate. When she returned with a leash and gently put it around Ami's neck, the dog didn't think much of it - Ami was accustomed to the practice. But panic grew in the pit of Ami's stomach when she was led to a car and lifted inside. She whined at the woman, who responded with more affection.

"No, no! My babies!" Ami cried in horror as she watched the road to her children fade away through the moving car's back window.

10

Present Day

Hours away from the pack, Layla scanned the area in all directions. She tried to keep her thoughts focused on food and off the prospect of an attack on her friends by feral dogs while she was gone. The Sloughi knew Ami and Brodie would fight their hearts out if it came to it, but she doubted either could overpower hardened street dogs.

Layla picked up speed when she spotted houses ahead, but she tried not to get her hopes up as she neared the buildings. She managed to suppress her feelings of panic, but they were growing stronger. Layla felt the anxiety burble in the pit of her stomach, but she couldn't afford to give in to the jitters.

Slowly, Layla cautiously walked through the streets. She stopped and surveyed the area. There were many houses but no cars, and it felt dead. There was no life, no movement, and nowhere to hide if there were hostile dogs around.

Scanning further, Layla couldn't even find a scruffy cat lapping at a leaky irrigation pipe. Life had never been here: the buildings stood uniformly empty, there was no glass in the windows, and no noise at all. "No life means no food," Layla sighed in defeat.

The frustrated dog struggled to keep her panic at bay. *No point dwelling here,* she mused, as if trying to give herself a pep talk.

Where to now? Layla wondered as she looked around. The ghost town was the first sign of human existence she'd seen in hours. Layla wondered how much energy she had left to continue the search. The pack leader needed a reserve to get back to the others, but how could she return without food for them?

Layla threw her nose up in the air and took a long, deep breath, then set off in the direction of the ocean.

* * * * *

"How much longer? I'm gonna dieeeee."

The whiney little dog's complaint challenged Ami's attempt to keep a grip on her nerves. Ami counted the minutes Layla had been away - not because she was so hungry, but because she was terrified something happened to her friend.

The stark memories of being taken away from her puppies had never faded. Ami thought about them every day: *What became of them? Did they survive? What did they think when I didn't return? They must have been so scared.*

Ami sighed and replied, "Not much longer, I'm sure."

Mia wasn't listening. She was attempting to chase down the fly that had been pestering her. The tiny greyhound jumped, turned sharply, and excitedly snapped at the air.

Brodie hopped close to Ami and flopped down on the dirt next to her. "What if she doesn't come back?" he asked.

Ami kept her gaze dead ahead. She didn't want to see Brodie's worried face, but more than that, she didn't want him to see hers. "She'll come back," the Saluki reassured.

Brodie motioned as if he was about to reply but stopped himself.

* * * * *

The trio hadn't said more than a few words to one another for the past twenty-four hours. The hunger they felt was all-consuming, and focusing on anything else was hard work. It was Ami who broke the silence early the following morning. "We've got to find food."

The hunger finally became too much for the gentle dog to bear, and idle time allowed sombre thoughts to creep into her mind. Layla's absence stretched far longer than any of them expected. And with it, Ami faced a reality that terrified her - she was a mother figure within the pack, but she was no leader.

The snappy response Ami anticipated from Mia never came. Instead, the little grey dog kept her eyes closed and her chin down. "Mia," Ami prompted.

Mia slowly opened one eye and gave Ami a sideways glance. "What if

Layla comes back?" she timorously questioned.

Brodie was the first to answer. "One of us should stay put."

Ami shook her head. "No, we stay together. No splitting up. Layla will find us if… when she comes back."

Brodie could tell from Ami's expression that the subject wasn't up for discussion. Both his and Mia's ears pricked up at the last part of Ami's utterance. They looked at each other but said nothing. Ami motioned to the one area they hadn't searched, as according to Mia, it had looked "too doggy." This time, Mia didn't object, and they all headed out.

Mia was right. Dogs definitely frequented the place. The smells alarmed them all, and they kept their eyes peeled for danger.

"This is really risky. I only smell dogs. I don't smell any food," whispered Brodie to Ami as she slowed to a halt.

"Keep going; there has to be something," she replied with poorly-feigned hope.

As they searched fruitlessly, the fearful hounds became more frantic. The prospect of starving to death seemed a whole lot more real.

"What are we going to do?" cried Mia, stomping and circling in panic.

"Shhhhhh!" Ami and Brodie both hissed at the trembling, glassy-eyed dog.

"What are we going to do?" Mia whined again, ignoring the order.

"Let's go back." Ami worried the tiny greyhound's yells would draw unwanted attention. The second-in-command turned to lead the pack back to their camp and stopped dead in her tracks.

A hundred metres ahead, two large dogs stood and stared straight at Ami and her friends. She could tell from the combative stances an attack was imminent.

In an uncharacteristic move, Ami growled, "Enough is enough!" She wouldn't run; she wouldn't back down. Ami would fight!

The furious Saluki charged the two hulking hounds, baring her teeth and growling as viciously as the gentle dog could. The two intruders did the same, running at Ami with teeth gnashing ferociously.

A hard shoulder budge came from behind, and Ami tumbled off course before she entered the fray. She righted herself and looked up to see Brodie run full pelt toward the savage hounds.

"No, Brodie, no!" Ami screamed in horror as she watched the three-legged boy throw himself into a fight he could never win. The two dogs descended on the tri-paw as he growled and thrashed and fought to stay on his feet.

"Layla! Layla! Help us!" Mia cried hopelessly for their absent leader, frantically circling behind Ami.

Brodie shrieked with pain as one dog sunk his teeth into his shoulder while the other pulled at his bad back leg. The agony provoked a brutal flashback to another moment of excruciating pain.

11

Brodie's Story

Brodie looked up at his weeping friend. The injured dog couldn't move, and he didn't want to try. He was in too much pain. Laying near the road, Brodie was completely still, except for a trembling that would not ease.

The roan-colored animal watched as a small crowd of familiar faces assembled around him. They put down a bedsheet and moved his smashed body onto it using all available hands. Brodie cried and felt Arlan's comforting hand resting gently on his head. Shuffling slowly, the group moved Brodie into the house and up to Arlan's bedroom. His human friends set the broken Azawakh down on his bed and left.

"I'm so sorry, Brodie. I'm so sorry."

Why is Arlan sorry? That confused Brodie - Arlan hadn't hit him; the metal monster did. Brodie managed to nudge his master's hand, and Arlan moved his bedclothes onto the floor beside the wounded dog. They laid there together all night, but Brodie's pain ensured neither got any rest.

Brow furrowed, Arlan paced and talked on his phone for hours the next morning. When the man suddenly left the room, Brodie kept his eyes on the door until Arlan reappeared. Arlan returned with an unfamiliar lady, and she slowly approached Brodie and touched him gently on the head, making soft cooing sounds.

The stranger and Arlan grabbed the corners of Brodie's blanket and used it as a stretcher to lift him off the floor. Carefully the pair maneuvered Brodie out of the house and into a car, where another stranger met them.

The injured animal was carried into a room at their destination and put on a cold, metal table. *This place smells funny,* Brodie thought as a stern-faced woman poked, prodded, and moved his legs. Everything hurt, but Brodie was too scared to make a noise as the brusque lady examined his back. He laid there quietly, gazing up at Arlan with pleading in his eyes. "Make it stop," the dog whimpered.

The pokey lady did something that made him feel better and a bit sleepy, and as Brodie closed his eyes, he saw Arlan leave the room, tears still running down his face.

That smell. Brodie's heart sank as soon as he woke. He wasn't home - nothing was familiar, and he was still in a horrible place. Arlan was gone, and Brodie didn't recognise anybody.

Why can't I move? the Azawakh wondered. Brodie tried to stand but couldn't. He tried to scrabble along the floor, but it was just as fruitless, and it hurt. It really hurt.

In constant pain, Brodie scrabbled around on the floor, and weeks went by without progress. Brodie's only comfort came from Arlan's visits, but the injured hound couldn't understand why his master didn't take him home.

Why do I have to be in this horrible place? Why aren't the other people like Arlan? Brodie brooded. The strangers just stepped over him, and they never touched or talked to him. *Is this my life now?* Brodie thought to himself every day.

One day, a new lady arrived. She crouched down and cooed and stroked Brodie gently, then she took photos of him and tapped on her phone for a while. The woman talked loudly at some of the staff, who barely responded, but she kept talking anyway. Then she left.

After that, things started to change. Brodie got more visits. The new lady with the phone came back a few times, and so did the other woman who helped Arlan get him to the vet clinic. None of them looked happy. In fact, they looked angry, and they spoke in harsh tones that worried Brodie. The people took photos of him and pointed at Brodie's damaged body - his broken hip and paralysed foreleg.

Two days later, when Brodie groggily woke up from a long sleep, he saw Arlan. His master was accompanied by the first lady, who he came to know as Lilian. The pair talked to the people around them again, but not as loudly or as harshly as before.

Brodie felt different. His hip felt different: it still really hurt but in a different way.

Suddenly, Arlan scooped Brodie up in his arms and headed to the door. The dog's heart beat harder with excitement. Was this it? Was he going home at last?

Brodie's excitement was short-lived. The car pulled into a driveway, and Brodie was carried into a new house. He could smell other dogs - a lot of them. The Azawakh's stomach jumped into his throat as Brodie looked around and realised he was in the middle of a pack - one to which he did not belong. One that did not know him.

This is going to be bad, Brodie thought as he kept his gaze low to the floor.

His fear slowly eased as a sea of wagging tails, sniffing noses, and wriggling dogs surrounded him. Unthreatened by his presence, the curious pack welcomed Brodie.

Arlan sat with Brodie for a while, then said goodbye and left. Brodie would see him three more times and then never again.

Excited to meet the new dog, the pack immediately knew something was wrong with their guest.

"Hi." Ami was the first to speak.

"Hello," Brodie nervously replied, despite the warm welcome.

"What happened to you?" Ami continued to talk.

"I got hit by a metal monster."

Ami's eyes widened. "And now you can't walk?"

"I guess. I mean, I try, but… it doesn't seem to happen," Brodie quietly answered.

Ami didn't know what to say, but when she noticed that Layla stood on the periphery, Ami turned the subject away from metal monsters.

"So, you're staying here then? With us?" Layla questioned.

It was clear that the black dog was pack leader. He wasn't sure what answer she would be happy with, so Brodie shrugged and cracked an uncomfortable smile.

"Well, it's pretty cool here. Lilian and Tom are really nice. They give us food every single day. Twice! And we all go out running togeth..." Ami caught herself a little too late.

Brodie bowed his head, and his eyes fell on the leg that no longer seemed to work.

"They take good care of us, and they'll take good care of you too," the gentle brown Saluki comforted, but Ami felt sad. She always took newbies under her wing and made them feel better, but she didn't know what to do with Brodie. She stayed next to him on the floor and looked up at the rest of the pack.

"Come on, guys," she quietly encouraged, as the rest of the dogs moved closer and laid down, surrounding Brodie. Ami hoped their acceptance would make Brodie feel better, and when she saw the way he looked at the dogs all around him, she knew she had been right.

* * * * *

Lilian wiped away a tear. Brodie couldn't figure out why she cried so often. The woman would look at him with such sadness in her eyes, stroke him gently, and then cry and hug him. She did it a lot, and Brodie didn't know what to do, so he just licked Lilian's face and wagged his tail. Sometimes it made the lady giggle, and sometimes it made her cry harder.

Everyone seemed a bit sad - they watched Brodie move about the best he could, then they'd look at each other with serious faces.

Each day Brodie tried to get up and run, but it wouldn't happen. His left legs refused to work - he could step forward a little, but that was all. It got him moving, but mostly the human-folk helped him around.

Weeks went by, and Brodie's new parents carted him all over town to vet upon vet, all of them poking, prodding, and "hmm'ing." Every time they left a clinic, Lilian would go quiet. She would sit with Brodie for a while when they got home, deep in thought as she gently stroked his bad legs. The hound had no idea why, but he enjoyed the company. He remained in good spirits while he healed, but the gangly dog yearned for his independence.

One day, Brodie woke up feeling a bit stronger. His hip didn't hurt too much anymore, and the rest of his body felt better. After a few attempts, he managed to rock himself up and into a standing position. His back left leg felt weak and odd, so he held it high off the ground and used his semi-paralysed front leg to steady himself as he hurtled forward.

It was a funny-looking gallop with only his right side working properly, but Brodie didn't care. He was moving! He was finally moving without any help. The injured dog hopped around the dining room and lounge as the other dogs watched him negotiate tables and chairs. They looked at each other and then back at him.

The freckled Azawakh hopped around until he started to tire. It was at this point, Brodie realised he didn't quite know how to stop, but he couldn't stand still. He had to keep his momentum to stay upright.

When Brodie spotted his bed, he made a beeline for it, and just as he did, Lilian and Tom appeared. They gasped and stopped in their tracks as they watched their newest pack member hurtle toward his bed. It wasn't a graceful landing, but Brodie couldn't have cared less. He buzzed with excitement. For the first time in nine weeks, he moved unassisted!

Lilian and Tom descended on the tired dog, giddy with happiness. *There are the tears again,* thought Brodie, as he looked up and licked Lilian's face. The injured dog stopped for a second. These were different tears. She wasn't sad - Lilian was smiling and crying. *Humans are so odd,* Brodie happily mused.

Weeks went by, and Brodie grew stronger and more confident. He slowly started to use his bad back leg. Although it would never be the same, the injured leg took some of his weight. Combined with his semi-paralysed front leg, getting about became relatively easy.

Lilian and Tom started to take Brodie out to the beach with the others, and Brodie loved this. In his element, Brodie ran with Layla, sniffed things with Ami, and buzzed past Mia to annoy her. He needed a little help from Lilian and Tom to get into the car, but other than that, he was his own man again.

Life went on while Brodie's back leg continued to improve and hold more weight, but his front leg did not heal. When some sensation returned to Brodie's toes, Lilian's hopes arose, but the dog's front leg did not regain any more of its former use.

* * * * *

Lilian took off Brodie's protective bandage and found a nasty, gunky mess under his dewclaw. The concerned woman motioned to Tom. "What's going on here?"

"That doesn't look good," said Tom as he investigated the sore. They cleaned it up and discovered a swollen, angry bump. "Let's see what it looks like in the morning," he comforted.

Lilian woke early to check on the Azawakh's paw. "Tom! It's much worse than it was last night!" Pus oozed from the sore, and it was a lot larger.

Brodie couldn't feel it, so he wasn't bothered.

Shocked at how quickly the infection progressed, Lilian and Tom rushed Brodie to the clinic. And one look at the vet's face confirmed their fears.

When Brodie gazed at Lilian's face, he saw tears. *Those aren't the happy ones,* he thought to himself.

After a weirdly quiet evening at home, an uneasy Brodie followed Lilian and Tom into the vet clinic early the next morning. He wasn't worried. These trips usually involved some touchy-feely stuff, and then they'd all go home. Brodie was more concerned about the fact that they forgot his breakfast.

However, when Lilian and Tom left, Brodie began to worry: *That isn't normal. Usually, they stay right here with me. Why are they leaving?*

* * * * *

"Brodie, you're okay, my angel, you're okay," Lilian crooned.

Brodie could hear Lilian, but his eyes were too heavy to open. He felt her kiss his nose and rest a hand gently on his neck, but Brodie didn't feel like moving. He was glad his mum came back, but the Azawakh really wanted to sleep. And Lilian's voice became distant as he drifted off.

The next day, Brodie woke in his cage with a shock as he struggled to remember where he was. He looked around for his pack, for Lilian, Tom, anyone familiar, then Brodie noticed the man coming toward him.

It took Brodie a little while, but the dog realised he remembered the guy. He met him a few times before when Lilian and Tom took him for examinations and x-rays.

"Howsit Brodie, how you doing?" The voice was familiar and comforted Brodie a little, but not much. He wanted to be back home with his pack where he belonged.

The man opened the cage and clipped a leash onto Brodie's collar.

Brodie went to push himself up and realised he couldn't. His leg wasn't working at all. The hound looked down and froze. *Where is it?* Alarmed, he looked up and back down again. No, it wasn't a dream. His leg was gone! In its place were bandages and a small plastic tube.

"Come on, Brodie. You can do it. You can get up," the man encouraged with a gentle tug on the leash as Brodie tried again.

Brodie maneuvered himself up using his other front leg and stepped out. He wanted to stop to investigate his missing limb, but he wanted out of that cage too. *I'm dying for a pee,* he silently exclaimed.

Carefully, Brodie hopped forward, feeling out the limits of his new body. He never really used the paralysed leg to walk or run; he just stabilised himself with it if he wobbled. To accommodate for the absence of the foreleg, Brodie put more weight on his weak back leg, and it was okay. It didn't hurt, and it didn't buckle.

With a few more steps, Brodie was outside. The sun felt good, and for a few moments, he stood and peed, his head pointed to the sky, taking in the glorious warmth. After a little time to sniff as much of the grass as possible, Brodie was led back inside.

It took some encouragement to get Brodie back into the cage, but he still felt weak and woozy, so he quickly laid back down to rest.

"Brodie! Oh, my Brodie-boy!" Lilian couldn't contain herself when she saw him.

Brodie looked up and saw her and Tom sporting broad smiles. The friendly man from before opened the cage, and Brodie stepped out to amazed expressions and congratulatory noises from Tom and Lilian.

Lilian beamed as she embraced the hound she missed so much over the past three days.

Brodie was ecstatic to be reunited with two of his family members, but he also really needed to pee again, so he was grateful to be led back out to the garden. He looked around at the row of smiling faces watching him do his business and cooing at every step. *Weirdos!* he thought.

For a moment, Ami watched, totally bewildered. Brodie fought with all of his heart, attacking both dogs at the same time to keep them focused on him. The Azawakh's spirit had always been stronger than his ability, and this time was no exception. Brodie ferociously spun, jumped, and thrashed without stopping for breath.

"Run! Go! Run now!"

As soon as Ami heard his commands, she realised Brodie knew he could not win the battle. The courageous hound was determined to sacrifice himself and give them a chance to get away.

Ami glanced back at a wide-eyed Mia and scanned the area. She would have to leave the tiny defenseless greyhound unguarded to help Brodie.

A loud, gargled scream forced Ami's decision, and she hurtled toward her three-legged ally. Using her substantial weight to her advantage, Ami smashed into the dogs, sending all three flying apart.

One attacker tumbled off his feet, so Brodie seized the opportunity to pin the dog down. The Azawakh struggled to get purchase with his lone front paw, and though he stumbled, Brodie kept the dog immobilised while Ami descended on the other aggressor.

Well aware the mongrels refused to admit defeat and slink off; Ami realised she and Brodie were at a significant disadvantage. It would be a fight to the death.

All the while, she could hear Mia screaming for Layla. *Mia is so loud for such a small dog,* Ami thought.

Finally, Brodie's adversary got to his feet and knocked his lame opponent down. The Azawakh was slow to get back up, and Brodie helplessly watched as the vicious dog ran toward the little greyhound.

Mia's shrieking fell silent, and she froze in horror as the bloodied dog hurtled toward her. A severely injured Brodie lolloped behind the enemy as fast as his broken body would allow.

"No!" Ami screamed as she glanced away from her own fight to watch the scene unfold. As she tried to run toward Mia, she felt teeth sink into her flank and pull her over.

"Run! Mia! Run!" Yelling was all Brodie and Ami could do, but Mia was frozen to the spot with fear. She closed her eyes, held her breath, and braced herself for the impact.

It never came. Mia heard a thud and opened her eyes; then the little dog hissed out a breath as she looked to her right. The sleek black figure of their pack leader rolled and thrashed against the onslaught of the street dog.

Layla was on her way back when she heard Mia's screams, and the exhausted Sloughi picked up the pace. Mia's yells renewed Layla's energy as she bound onto the scene and took out the enormous male. The cur's nearly lethal attack on the most helpless member of their pack enraged Layla, and the anger pushed her to fight harder than she'd ever fought before.

Unrelenting, Layla ferociously shredded the dog, forcing him to turn and flee for his life. Without mercy, she pursued and easily caught the animal, knocking him head-over-heels.

Taking full advantage of the brute's disorientation, Layla seized the opportunity to clamp down on the mongrel's throat. He struggled to free himself, flipping around, gargling, and trying to draw breath. Layla's eyes bulged as she felt the body go limp. She opened her jaw and looked at the lifeless, bloodied dog. Panting loudly, Layla turned and ran at the last assailant, rage still burning in her eyes.

Successful in the battle against Ami and Brodie, the female attacker turned and fled when her mate fell at the Sloughi's feet.

Layla sprinted past her pack mates to chase down the fleeing female.

"Layla! It's over! Layla, stop!" Ami urged.

Layla wasn't listening. She ran until her lungs ached, but her target escaped – driven hard by fear. Journey-weary before the battle, Layla's desire for blood lost out to her buckling legs.

* * * * *

"He's dead."

Layla returned to her packmates as they stood around the lifeless body, with heads bowed. "I know," she answered with a faint air of impudence.

There was much to say, but no one spoke. Layla looked around – she could see it in their faces and knew what they were thinking. Her gaze fell to a small pool of blood that gathered underneath Brodie's chest - the deep puncture wounds a testament to his brave battle. The Sloughi glanced at the leg Ami held up – the vicious bite causing pain whenever the gentle dog put weight on it. "They wouldn't have stopped until you were all dead," Layla calmly commented.

It was an explanation none of them needed, and no one replied.

Layla's exhaustion effectively hid her shock, and she struggled to come to terms with the enormity of what happened. But, the pack leader found comfort in the realisation that she could do what was necessary to protect her family.

And, it was important for her pack to know the dangers they faced. Layla began to assess their situation. "How badly are you hurt, Brodie?"

"I'm fine."

"He's not fine; he can barely move," the greyhound mumbled.

Brodie shot Mia a glance that told her he did not appreciate the input.

Seeing Brodie's reluctance to face reality, Layla didn't ask anymore. "We all need to rest. Let's find somewhere and bed down for the night."

Everyone but Mia tried to hide their winces as they slowly searched for a spot tucked away from the main drag and harsh reality – a safe place away from the stark, bloody reminder that still laid out in the open.

Morale at an all-time low, the three big dogs sat for a while - silently licking their wounds and lapping at each other when someone couldn't reach a sore spot.

It had been days since they'd eaten anything bar a few barely edible scraps.

Never one to have much compassion, Mia looked at her hungry, battered pack with new eyes. *I am a burden,* she morosely acknowledged to herself. *I can't fight, or track, or do any of the things they know how to do,* the little greyhound thought in frustration. Mia knew she would be dead without her friends, and she felt useless. Though those ideas wouldn't have bothered her one jot before, suddenly, it was a weight she struggled to carry.

Mia watched quietly as her three protectors dropped off to sleep one by one. The silence gave the tiny greyhound time to think. She had to be useful! There had to be something she could do - something that would make her a valuable member of the pack. With that in mind, Mia waited until they were all fast asleep and made her exit.

* * * * *

Ami's nose twitched. *What is that smell?* the Saluki groggily wondered. The gentle dog slowly opened her eyes to a sight that led her to believe she was still asleep: a bleary-eyed but happy little grey dog sat beside a large stash of what could only be described as semi-edible objects.

Mia puffed out her chest as she watched the big brown dog take stock of the offering.

"What on earth? Where did you get all this? *You* did this?" Ami had so many questions, and Mia was very ready to answer, but the greyhound wanted to wait until she had their leader's attention.

Mia wanted Layla's approval so badly that she hadn't eaten a morsel of the bounty herself. It took enormous restraint, but she wanted Layla to see her "winnings" in all their glory.

Oblivious to the little dog's agenda, Ami moved towards the pile.

"No, not yet!" Mia urged and looked at the black dog, still deep in sleep.

Ami looked to where Mia's gaze dropped and caught on. It took Ami a few nudges to get the black dog awake.

Layla cracked one eye open, then the other, and turned her head toward the early morning pest with her customary deadpan look.

Ami nodded toward the expectant little dog who found it hard to sit still.

Layla said nothing. She slowly got up and walked over to the collection Mia amassed. The pack leader rooted around cautiously, inspecting and pushing pieces about with her nose. "Where did you get all this?"

Hoping for more of a reaction, a slightly deflated Mia began her tale. "Well, you know how Lilian and Tom always used to watch you guys on walks because they were so worried that you'd run away or get onto a road? Well, they never watched me because I would *never* have done that."

Layla shot a sideways glance at Ami.

Mia noticed the look and explained, "No, no! What I mean is, because they weren't watching me, I used to sneak into those little huts up on those mounds we walked across. I think humans used to live in those things because sometimes there was food in them. Lilian and Tom never knew about it. So, I went to look, and sure enough, I found biscuits! They're old, but they smell okay."

Suitably impressed, Ami looked at the little dog - half lamenting the fact she never looked in those huts herself.

Mia continued, "I also remembered those fires people had on the beaches on the weekends. They almost always left food behind, bones mostly." She gestured to a charred lamb shank and an array of chicken bones. "And then I remembered that place that mum used to scowl at - that place with the falcons and the pigeons. Remember? She would look at all the poor dismembered birds on the ground and tut. Well, now we have pigeon bits for breakfast too!" Mia was finished and looked to Layla with expectant eyes.

The black dog with the tan features stepped slowly forward and moved a few of the scraps around.

Their leader's extended pause dampened Mia's excitement somewhat, and she looked to Ami for support. Ami gazed back and, with a slow blink, told the little dog to be patient.

Layla peered up and into the distance. "Nice one," she said, shooting a brief glance at Mia, who breathed a sigh of relief.

"Tuck in!" the ecstatic greyhound rejoiced, and she and Ami began to pick out the biscuits from the pile.

"Wait for Brodie, you two; he's still asleep."

As soon as Layla said it, they all stopped and looked at the motionless body in their sleeping area. They all knew it was weird for him to be the last up. Brodie was an early riser - so early, in fact, that the pack constantly ordered him back to bed in the wee hours when he wanted to go and wake Lilian for breakfast.

"How badly was he hurt?" Layla asked as they all ignored their hunger and slowly walked over to their brother. There was no movement from him.

"Look at his breathing." Mia watched his chest strain as it heaved up and down. "That doesn't seem right."

Ami laid down at Brodie's head and nudged his cheek gently. There was no response. She repeatedly prodded the Azawakh until Ami panicked and pushed her nose hard against his.

Brodie's eyes opened. He squinted in the sunlight as the three figures surrounding him came into focus. "Oh, hey guys."

Relieved, Ami stood up. "Brodie, how are you feeling?"

Not making any effort to get up, Brodie attempted cheerfulness. "Oh, you know, I've been better."

Layla looked the downed dog over and motioned. "Is it that leg?"

Brodie looked back at the leg damaged by the metal monster. It was never quite right after that, and he grudgingly answered, "I'm afraid so."

Ami hung her head. "You should have stayed away. I could have handled it." She half scolded and half wept. Overwhelmed by guilt, the gentle Saluki moaned, "If I hadn't taken them on, you wouldn't have tried to help me."

Mia comforted the big brown dog in her squeaky manner, "You didn't have a choice!"

"Mia's right; they weren't going to back down." Layla sternly reassured.

Ami's head hung as she moved closer to Brodie to look at his beaten and bloodied body. "Can you stand?" she whispered.

Solemnly, Brodie shook his head.

Ami whimpered. It was all too much for her. When Lilian and Tom brought Brodie home, it was Ami who stayed by his side, Ami who kept his spirits up when he couldn't walk, Ami that accompanied Brodie to every single vet visit, and Ami that nursed him through the amputation. She stayed positive throughout that entire period, but this fresh blow was too much for the sweet companion to bear.

Unsure what to do, Layla stood and looked at her broken friends, then to Mia and the pile of scraps.

Mia understood and gathered the bounty up for Brodie. If he was to have any chance at all, he needed to eat.

Once she pulled herself together, Ami joined a pensive Layla a few metres away. "It's something at least. Mia really tried, and she's talking about going on another scavenge," Brodie's guardian whispered. "But it's not going to be enough."

Layla shook her head. "He needs proper food. I need to leave again."

Ami took a sharp breath. The prospect of being left alone with two dogs to protect made the Saluki's blood run cold, but she understood there was little choice.

"I'll take Mia with me," the black dog commented.

Ami looked at Layla, bemused. Layla shot an equally bemused expression back to her. There was logic in her decision, but she still wasn't over the moon about spending one-on-one time with the most annoying member of their pack.

13

"Will they be long?" Brodie asked.

Ami tried to keep from thinking about it. "I don't know, Brodie. I hope not." She battled to keep her anxiety at bay and fought even harder to keep it from showing.

Ami kept her nose high to pick up any alarming scents and slowly patrolled the area. After three perimeter checks, Ami decided she was overly worried and started to walk back to Brodie, who was too weak to stay awake for any amount of time.

She was a few steps away from her injured friend when Ami froze, her almond eyes becoming wide and round. The Saluki didn't make a sound. She raised her nose in the air and breathed deeply. *There it is again! Unmistakable,* Ami realised. She slowly turned and spotted two figures in the distance, staring straight at their camp.

Ami looked back at Brodie, who sensed the fear in Ami and was now wide awake. He looked at her with trepidation in his eyes and slowly shook his head. They both knew they wouldn't survive another fight. Ami looked back at the intruders: they weren't barking, they weren't growling, but they were standing their ground.

Ami racked her brain, wishing it was Layla's instead of her own. She walked a few steps toward the dogs and stopped. They mirrored her movement. The Saluki's heart sank as the small hope that they were just passing through disappeared. A fight was imminent, and Ami was terrified.

When Brodie realised Ami's intention, he whispered, "No, use your voice."

That idea hadn't occurred to Ami - she was an unusually quiet dog who rarely even whimpered. She'd never tried to use her voice to intimidate anyone, and as this realisation dawned on her, she started to growl.

"Louder!" Brodie called in encouragement.

Ami pulled her lips back and growled with all the ferociousness she could muster.

The mongrels took a step back but kept their eyes on the snarling hound in front of them.

Brodie watched in wonder. He had never seen Ami this way. "Keep going!" he cheered, emboldening Ami to growl louder and louder until the snarls became an ear-piercing bark.

Brodie and the hostile intruders were all taken aback. "Yes, Ami! Keep going; it's working!"

The dogs took another few steps backward but still refused to retreat. Ami's eyes fell to Layla's kill. Resolutely, the big Saluki slowly moved toward the corpse, doing her best to imitate Layla's predatory, menacing gait. When Ami reached the reeking carcass, she put a paw on the body, her stance fierce and proud.

That was enough for the uninvited guests. As soon as the curs' eyes dropped to the torn, bloodied body, they withdrew with bowed heads and downcast eyes. Ami held her defiant pose until they were out of sight and then collapsed to the ground with an enormous sigh.

"That. Was. Amazing!" Brodie's eyes were wide and excited.

The amiable Saluki looked around, visibly shaken and bewildered.

"Ami, that was… that was just amazing!"

Unable to join in Brodie's elation, she sighed, "That was far too close." Eyes pinned on the horizon and nose in the air, she sat next to Brodie. "Get some rest."

* * * * *

"Where are we going?" It was the third time Mia asked, and Layla still hadn't heard.

Focused on the guilt and anger left over from the attack on her pack, Layla felt responsible for the injuries that threatened Brodie's life. But her friends were alone and vulnerable again as she vigorously renewed the hunt.

Layla ignored her injuries, and she pushed through the pain until she felt them no more. The big black Sloughi was determined to make up for what she saw as a failure to keep them all safe.

She led Mia to the flood plains in between the two beaches they knew well. It was a vast expanse of rough, dried, salty sand with occasional patches of brush. Layla stopped dead and dropped to the ground, quickly looking back at Mia to ensure the noise-bag didn't utter a word.

For once, Mia stayed quiet and dropped down next to Layla. The tiny greyhound knew that falling in line and obeying directions was imperative, now more than ever.

Mia followed Layla's line of sight and saw a large herd of goats. She looked at Layla, then back at the goats, then glanced back at Layla. "Wait, are we... going to...?"

Layla looked at Mia and nodded.

"How?" the tiny dog wondered out loud. Mia waited for Layla to survey the land in front of them. The open area was flat and devoid of any opportunity to corral the goats. "This isn't going to be easy," she grumbled.

Frustrated, the Sloughi considered the problem. Herding was not something Layla knew how to do - she was not a shepherd. She was a high-speed hunter that ran down individual prey. And that skill could work now, but Layla was rusty, exhausted, and injured. She hadn't chased down anything larger than a seabird in many years!

Mia isn't going to be much help either, the leader inaudibly sighed. The itty-bitty greyhound was pretty fast, but taking down a goat would likely cause Mia serious injury. However, Mia was noisy. Maybe the hyperactive dog's annoying yelling could prove useful after all.

"That one." Layla's eyes fell on a straggler, an older goat that couldn't keep up with the rest. Layla noticed the animal on her first trip out. She carefully watched to see if it was sick or just old, and it appeared to be the latter.

Mia looked at Layla with expectant eyes. How exactly was she, with all her six kilos, supposed to help in this endeavour?

"I'll run it down, but if that herd decides to come at me, I'll need you to scare them off. I'll need you to shout louder than you've ever shouted before," Layla directed.

Confidently, Mia nodded, despite the growing dread in the pit of her stomach. The prospect of using nothing but her shrill yap to stave off thirty-odd angry goats made the greyhound stare blankly at her leader.

"Mia! Focus! This is really important."

Mia knew it. The meagre scraps Mia found barely kept them alive, and now they had Brodie to consider. She knew how important it was to get her packmate proper food if he was going to survive. Mia felt the pressure of the situation and understood a little more why Layla was always so serious, so focused.

"Stay close, but stay behind me," Layla commanded.

The two hounds slowly set off toward the herd. Layla got into position. She waited and looked around one last time, then bolted at full speed toward the group. The goats started to panic when the first animal saw the black dog approach.

As Layla predicted, they ran, leaving the old goat far behind. She chose her moment and seized the goat by the back leg, toppling it over onto the dusty ground. The billy started to yell, which shocked Mia, and she looked toward the rest of the herd, terrified of a stampede.

The determined little greyhound got into position, puffed her chest out, and shot her tail upright. She watched with palpable relief as none of the herd came back for their fallen comrade, and silence fell as Layla quickly finished the job. Mia trotted over and looked at the still body of the goat. She looked at Layla, and Layla looked right back at her for once. They both felt terrible about their actions - they knew the goat wanted to live, the same way they did. But, desperation led them to it.

"Brodie," Mia said softly but firmly, and Layla appreciated the reminder.

While the other goats looked on from a distance, Layla took a leg in her mouth and began the laboured journey back to the others, wishing that Mia was a heftier dog.

14

"How is he?" panted an exhausted Layla as she dropped the goat on the ground near the sleeping area.

"I don't think he's letting on how bad it is," replied a solemn Ami, still racked with inescapable guilt.

Layla bent to pick the goat back up but was immediately stopped by her gentle-faced friend. "Let me. Please," Ami requested.

Layla obliged, knowing it was important for Ami and because she could barely take another step. Ami dragged the carcass to where Brodie was lying.

"Oh my gosh!" he exclaimed when he saw the bounty. He looked at Layla and Mia with a huge smile plastered across his face and his characteristic tip-of-the-tail wag.

Layla was happy to see his spirits were still high.

Brodie looked at the goat and then up at the others. "How do I...?"

Layla shot a bemused glance at Ami, who walked over to sit beside Brodie and made a start. As she got through to the flesh, Ami tore pieces off for Brodie to gobble up, which he did without hesitation.

"Feast until you can't fit any more in, Brodie," Layla commanded. She was thrilled he had an appetite. Ami's visible relief at assisting Brodie made Layla happy as well.

Layla's eyes dropped to the little grey scavenger that circled the area, and her face softened for a brief moment. Mia never waited for her turn, and Layla knew it took everything the little yipper had in her not to tuck in as well. But Mia had been brave, and she was starting to act like a true member of the pack.

After Brodie was full to bursting, he regaled Mia and a very concerned Layla with the tale of Ami's triumphant stand-off. With a huge smile on his face, the Azawakh spread out on his side with a distended belly that protruded from his bony frame.

His packmates took their turns to feed. It was a relief to eat without restraint, and it made them all giddy for a while. Once again, they were able to escape thoughts of their dire situation for a short time.

"Do you think she's back yet?" Mia asked, her words muffled by the hunk of meat she noisily chewed.

Oblivious to the weight of the question, Mia continued her meal. But everyone else paused, and they looked at each other - realising they hadn't considered that Lilian and Tom might return. Focused on food, water, and safety, they hadn't entertained the possibility.

With far fewer preoccupations, Mia was free to ponder life's mysteries as she chose and didn't seem to realise the effect of the thought she voiced. She noticed the silence though, and took a momentary break from filling her face, looking up at three sets of furrowed brows. "What?"

Layla looked at Ami. "They might be. They might be back," was the hopeful response the leader received from her best friend.

It dawned on Layla that she didn't have a plan. Not a long-term one anyway. Where were they actually going? Were they just aimlessly wandering, trying to stay alive, living on scraps and old goats, and fending off enemy attacks? It was a much better bet to trust that their humans would come back for them, but that meant a return to hostile territory, and the thought of more feline encounters made Layla's lips curl back on her teeth.

Knowing that their home was probably crawling with cats almost quashed the idea of going back to look for Lilian. Anything was preferable to facing Raven again, even carrying on into the vast nothingness.

The little grey dog realised she was onto something. "They could have come back. They could be looking for us, and we're out here in the middle of nowhere."

Layla took her time to look at the three expectant faces around her. The Sloughi paused before she subtly shifted her eyes to Brodie. She didn't need to say anything to make the hope in their faces disappear.

Ami hung her head, guilt clawing at her gentle soul. Brodie hadn't moved since the fight. Ravaged by grief over her protective companion's sacrifice, Ami tenderly questioned, "Brodie? Can you walk?"

Without a word, Brodie tightly clenched his jaw and rocked himself to his feet. The others stood and watched in silent anticipation of the first steps.

As Brodie cried out and crashed to the ground, Layla closed her eyes.

Ami rushed to comfort her injured friend as he groaned and winced in pain.

Their leader confirmed what they all knew: "We have to stay here."

"No."

"What?" Layla looked at Brodie, asking him to repeat himself.

There was determination in the Azawakh's tone. "No. You're not staying here."

"It's okay, Brodie, we…" Ami reassured.

Uncharacteristically, Brodie cut Ami off, "You have to leave me here and go back." The injured animal's eyes fixed on his leader.

Mia's uninhibited contributions often spelled out what the others avoided: "But what will happen to you? What if those dogs come back? How will you defend yourself?"

Layla continued the thought with a little more tact. "He's right. If he can't walk, he can't come with us. If we find Lilian and Tom, we can bring them back here to him."

Panic spread across Ami's soft face. "You can't be serious, Layla. Leave him here? On his own? What if the dogs come back? They know we're here! What if we can't get back to him? He'll starve to death! You can't be seriously considering this?"

It was the first time Ami ever spoke to Layla, or anyone for that matter, in such a way, and they were all taken aback. Layla faced many difficult decisions since their abandonment, but this one was by far the hardest. And it showed in her pained expression.

Ami kept her eyes fixed on the troubled black dog for some time before she softened her expression, realising it was her friend she was glaring at - the friend that carried the weight of the world on her shoulders.

For the first time, Layla didn't know what to do. The silence was deafening, and even the birds stopped singing in anticipation of the forthcoming decision. "Try again," she gently directed.

Brodie looked up at his leader, whose focus rested entirely on him.

Layla repeated the command. "Get up, and try again."

Brodie quickly understood the reason for the order. As much as Ami's gentle support comforted Brodie, it was Layla's tough love approach that pushed him that last mile when he yearned to walk. During his convalescence, Layla ran and jumped in front of him, not to taunt Brodie, as he first thought. No, the determined Sloughi pushed him to try harder, and that made the difference. And she was doing it again.

They all watched as the three-legged dog pushed himself up a second time. Brodie held his breath and fixed his gaze ahead as he moved forward. He winced and started to keel over.

Ami, who watched him like a hawk, immediately jumped up. Rooted to his side, Ami allowed the wobbly hound to push off her and re-balance himself.

The injured dog gazed at his faithful companion and managed a pained smile.

"You can do this," his gentle friend whispered.

With another ungainly step, Brodie found his balance. He looked at Layla, whose eyes hadn't left him for a second. Ami stayed beside Brodie for the next few steps, ready to catch him again. His winces lessened, and his pace increased as he took step after step, becoming more surefooted and smiling wider with every footfall. It wasn't long before he was quite a distance from the camp.

"Stop, come back now!" shouted Mia to her overjoyed packmate.

"No! Keep going, Brodie! Don't stop! We're coming!" It was the first time in a long time that there had been any joy in Layla's voice.

"Let's go!" Brodie enthusiastically agreed.

There was a sense of excitement and anticipation as they made their way back to town, but with it came trepidation. There was much to be mindful of: Lilian and Tom might still be absent. The cats would almost certainly have taken over the entire compound, and if not the cats, maybe more hostile dogs. But it still felt good to head toward some semblance of familiarity, and hope shone in every pair of eyes.

Layla carefully watched Brodie to make sure he didn't overdo it, as was his typical modus operandi. "Okay, stop. Let's rest," she decided.

They all plonked themselves down by the same mound they had slept next to on their first night and spread out on the sand.

After a short silence, Layla began her briefing. "We don't know what we're walking into." Eyes that previously scanned the scenery immediately focused on their leader. "Before we even consider searching for Lilian and Tom, we need to figure out what has happened to our home. Those disgusting felines have probably taken over," Layla grumbled.

"What then?" Mia interrupted, in keeping with her usual practice.

They all shot the greyhound a glance that told her to "be quiet and pay attention."

"Numbers," Layla continued. "We need to know how many there are.

If they're too numerous, we have to back out and find another way for Lilian and Tom to find us. If there aren't too many, maybe we can reclaim our place." Layla struggled to hide her shudder at the thought of cats all over her sofa.

"So, what's the plan?" Ami asked.

Layla turned to her friend. "You and me, Ami." Brodie's eyes widened, but he stayed silent. "Once we get to the outskirts of the compound, you and I head inside. Brodie and Mia will stay hidden in the bushes along the roadside."

Layla didn't address the other dogs directly for a reason: it wasn't their choice. She was telling them what to do without the opportunity to oppose her decision.

Brodie's eyes fell, his gaze on the fresh wounds that hampered his front leg. He could barely make it to the compound as it was, so he knew why Layla didn't include him in her plan. And he let his silence demonstrate compliance.

Mia was a little deflated by the exclusion, but the memory of Raven's attack stilled any protest.

Layla didn't go further into her plan. She knew Ami would follow her lead, so there was no need. "Let's rest here. We'll head out mid-morning."

There was logic in Layla's timing. If they set out in the morning, they would hit the compound at the warmest part of the day, and fewer felines would be on the prowl. They would be tucked away, escaping the heat.

15

Night fell on the pack, and it was a restless slumber. Aside from the thirst and the hunger that grew again, they were all painfully aware that finding Lilian and Tom was a long shot. The thought had all four dogs tossing and turning until daybreak.

Brodie was the first to wake. Despite being unsettled, he had rested for a long time, and his body felt markedly better. "I'm so thirsty."

Layla opened her eyes but didn't raise her head. There were two water sources they knew of: one guarded by dogs and one guarded by humans. Neither option appealed, but it was pretty much assured that any water source they could find would already be claimed and protected. *We can outrun humans more easily than dogs,* the Sloughi concluded. So, Layla got up, stretched, and prepared to head out. "We'll go to that grassy area opposite the compound."

Ami stumbled as she recalled the stinging whack she received the last time they were there. She swallowed her apprehension and followed her leader - this was not a time to show fear. They both had to be brave for Brodie and Mia, though Layla was far better at displaying the trait.

The primal pull to quench their thirst got the pack to the water source sooner than Layla anticipated. They stood and watched for any activity. There was none. Abundantly relieved, they each drank from a run-off puddle at the edge of the grass. The water replenished their energy and lifted their spirits.

Incredibly grateful for her renewed vigour, Layla commented, "We're a little early. Let's find a good hiding place for you two." The abundance of overgrown bushes alongside the road provided plenty of places to hide her weaker packmates. "Here." Layla motioned to a collection of shrubbery with ample space to stretch out, should her injured tri-pawed friend need a rest. "This will do. You have to stay here until we return."

"What if you don't?"

"Shut up, Mia!" Brodie snapped at the tactless little dog.

Mia looked at him, slightly shocked at the Azawakh's unusual demeanour.

Brodie accepted that he wasn't going to be able to help Layla and Ami, but it didn't sit well with him, and he was agitated. "Sorry," he said, once he realised he shocked his well-meaning companion.

"We're just going to look. Only needs two of us." Ami tried to comfort her dejected packmate. "It's nice to be back here." The gentle Saluki voiced what they were all thinking. The familiarity was a strange comfort, but a comfort nonetheless. Little did she know it, but Ami said exactly what her nervous friend needed to hear.

Layla was stoic in her composure, but inside, she struggled to keep it together. *There is so much riding on this mission,* she silently fretted. The big black dog was mentally exhausted. Her last few days took a toll, and the prospect of a feline face-off nearly pushed Layla over the edge. But Ami's heartfelt reminder was precisely what she needed to summon the last of her will. "This is our place. Let's go take back our home."

"Okay, so what's the plan?" Ami prompted.

Wryly, Layla stared at Ami and then back to the road.

"Okay, so we're winging it." Ami was never slow on the uptake. What plan could they conceive for a situation they never faced before? What preparations could they possibly make?

The duo trotted on until they reached the entrance to the compound. The hounds slowed to a walk but didn't stop for fear they'd lose their courage. Instinctively, they scanned the area in a cyclical, systematic manner; Layla covering the right, Ami the left. The place was unnervingly still. Layla slowed to a stop. Ami did the same.

"If it kicks off, you just run, okay? You get out of here and go back to them." Layla's eyes fixed ahead.

Ami paused, then tried to respond. "It's not going to kick…"

"Promise me." Layla fixed her eyes on Ami.

After another pause, followed by a reluctant nod from the brown dog, they headed deeper into the compound.

"I don't smell dog. At least, I don't smell fresh dog." Ami announced her observation quietly as they continued their cautious scan.

"Nor do I."

Neither one knew what to make of this. Did it mean the dogs left the compound? Or did it mean they never left the houses? As they approached home, their noses twitched as they searched for any scent that might reveal a threat. None of the pack would ever forget Raven's smell.

"The door's open." Ami knew Layla noticed, but she pointed it out to help her ally overcome the disgust that kept the Sloughi from advancing.

Layla took a long breath. "Let's go."

As soon as Layla's paw hit the driveway, the smell of cat hit her nose. She turned back to give Ami a brief look of disdain, then slowly walked inside the house. Ami stayed close behind.

They instinctively looked to the sofa where their pack spent hours sleeping, playing, and snuggling. Both expected to see it covered in cats, but the entire bottom floor of the house appeared deserted. There was no movement, no sound, no life.

Layla and Ami silently made a few patrols until they were satisfied no living creature remained. Puzzled but not reassured, they looked at each other in confusion. Their noses never failed. The house couldn't be cat-free. Could it?

Layla motioned to the stairs and, tentatively, began to ascend. She made no sound as she carefully placed each paw. She had always been incredibly surefooted. However, Ami had to concentrate to ensure she didn't clash a claw on the marble steps.

The lounge was clear, as were two of the three rooms, their doors wide open. The bathroom was clear too. The eyes of the investigating hounds fell to the third room, with its door slightly ajar. It was their bedroom - the place they all slept soundly with Lilian and Tom every night. And it was the source of feline stench that made their noses twitch. Layla positioned herself just outside and looked back at Ami. A supportive nod from the tense brown dog was all Layla needed to creep inside slowly.

She immediately saw a cat curled up on the foot of the bed. Though it was dim in the room, Layla could see it wasn't Raven. The tiny orange tabby had its short bobbed tail curved around its head.

Ami and Layla halted just inside the bedroom and fixed their eyes on the oblivious, sleeping moggy. Barely daring to breathe, Ami looked around the room while Layla kept her eyes on the bundle of orange fluff.

Ami froze as she clocked a pair of eyes watching her. She flinched when she spotted another pair, and then another. Ami slowly stepped closer to Layla. As she did so, she bumped a chair, which scraped the floor and woke the sleeping kitty. It jumped up, arched its back, and hissed at the pair of intruders.

Both Layla and Ami made for the door, but they pushed it closed in their blind panic, trapping themselves inside the room. Layla spun to meet the ambush head-on, and Ami followed suit.

Fear chased down Ami's spine as her eyes narrowed, but as her leader's rigid posture relaxed, the Saluki stared in confusion. Ami glanced at the cats, who blinked back.

As the hounds watched, more tabbies appeared, until the entire bed swarmed with cats. Yet, neither Layla nor Ami felt alarmed. There was no predatory feeling or sense of malevolence.

Layla and Ami watched in silence as more cats emerged from the wardrobe, the cupboards, and under the table to join their companions on the bed. They were all so thin, so weak, and so visibly defeated.

Ami lowered herself to the floor to show the cats they meant no harm as the standoff dissipated. She shot Layla a glance, imploring her to do the same. But that was a big ask for the black dog, so Layla returned an indignant look and remained standing. These cats meant no harm, but the Sloughi remained guarded.

Thankfully, Ami's gesture was enough to put the entire room more at ease and elicit a response from the tortoiseshell cat near the front of the bed. "Who are you?"

Layla may have looked calm, but she was seething. "Who are we? Who are you? This is our house!"

Ami cut in. "We… used to live here. This was our home."

The anxious cats looked at each other. Ami didn't notice any of the impudent looks she expected. Instead, the gentle dog saw their worry and fear. And it didn't sit well with her.

Layla saw it too. She expected a terse come-back, a confident claim to their property, but it never came.

"Okay. We'll leave." As the cats began to drop off the bed and head toward the door, Ami sadly looked to Layla with concern. It was clear that the starving cats had nowhere else to go.

Layla drew an audible breath. "Wait." The exodus froze. All eyes were on the expressionless black dog. "You don't have to go… yet. If you stay out of our way, maybe you can stay here for a while. Until you find somewhere else."

It was hard for Ami to gauge whether the cats were relieved or not. They slowly crept back to their original positions, but no one looked comfortable. The motherly dog wanted to know more. "What happened here? Why are you all in this one room? Why are you all so thin? Are there no mice or birds left?"

The tortoiseshell cat spoke again. "We can't hunt. We can't leave this house."

"Why?" Ami's tone was gentle. She never hated cats the way Layla did, and the ragged group made her feel sad.

"Raven," a kitten whimpered.

Layla's eyes widened at the mention of the name. "What do you mean?" she curtly asked.

"She… she takes our food. Whenever we hunt, she takes whatever we catch. There's an army of them. They kill everything in sight and keep it for themselves. If we catch or scavenge anything, they take it. Raven's spies are everywhere." The cats hung their heads as they listened to their friend explain.

Curious, Ami asked, "Why aren't you in her army?"

"We were. We left. We all left."

Inquisitive amber eyes searched the ragtag gathering. More softly, Layla questioned, "Why?"

A black and white cat jumped from the bed and walked toward the drawn curtain. He hooked the material with a paw, then moved backward, letting light cut through the dimness. As the cat returned to the bed, the sunlight revealed a limp that Ami missed before.

As she and Layla scanned each and every member of the dishevelled group, they spotted injury upon injury, old and new. Many of them had one closed or cloudy eye from being slashed in the face. A few held up limbs that wouldn't bear much weight. Almost all of them had shredded ears.

"Raven? Raven did this?" Layla rumbled.

The tortoiseshell cat nodded. "If we didn't follow orders, or if we didn't catch any mice or birds . . ."

A grey cat with a huge scar across her right eye cut in, "Or if she was just in a bad mood!" The feline spat the words like there was a bad taste in her mouth.

The tortoiseshell continued: "So, we left. Now we stay here, living like this, feeding on whatever we can find, and staying out of sight of Raven's patrols." At this, all heads lowered.

What a truly sorry sight, Ami thought.

The two dogs looked at each other, then back at the dejected collection of defeated felines huddled on the bed.

"Stay here," Layla said to Ami. But the utterance raised many hopeful heads, so Layla turned to the cats and repeated the command.

The big black dog turned to leave the room but stopped when she saw the door - the one that closed earlier as they panicked. Layla paused. She didn't want to ask for help from these animals, but she needed to get out.

Sheepishly, the dog shifted her eyes to the side and tipped her head slightly, avoiding eye contact with any of the cats. The subtle message conveyed, Layla watched as a tabby jumped off the bed and walked to the door. The helpful kitten jumped up and hooked herself onto the door handle, opening the latch. She squeezed a paw into the gap and pulled the door open.

Layla slowly bowed her head in appreciation and left.

16

While the black dog was off collecting the rest of the pack, Ami explained everything to the felines. So, when Layla returned with two more dogs in tow, the cats remained calm.

Still, Brodie couldn't help but stare wide-eyed at the invaders. It was a foreign feeling to be so close to so many cats. And it took everything Brodie had in him not to holler the "cat warning" that came so naturally to him.

"Mia, come." Ami anticipated the situation would be most difficult for the tiny grey dog. After all, Mia still bore the scars of her own encounter with the hellish feline they all feared.

Quivering just outside the door, Mia shook her head.

"Come. It's okay."

Ami's gentle voice reassured the little dog far more than Layla's brisk "briefing." Mia recalled the rundown from Layla: "Be warned. There are cats in the house. They won't attack though."

Staying close to her friends, Mia slowly crept forward until she stood next to Ami.

Relaxed, Ami gently encouraged, "Look at them."

Lifting her fearful gaze from her motherly packmate, Mia's narrowed eyes widened when she realised why Ami asked her to look at the huddled felines. The little greyhound saw the scars, shredded ears, and missing fur. The cats saw Mia's as well and realised they had a fellow Raven survivor in their midst.

A calmness descended on the room. Even Brodie's feelings of alarm withered away, and he let his guard down. It was evident they shared a nemesis, and it was clear they needed to help each other.

"Did any humans come here?" It hadn't dawned on Layla to ask yet, and she uttered the words quickly, as though catching up for lost time.

"No, no humans at all."

Hopes dashed, Layla motioned for her pack to leave the room. The hounds walked to the lounge, but no one got onto a sofa. It felt so alien to be home with Lilian and Tom's scent long gone.

In a hushed voice, Layla decided, "We have to take this place back." Her packmates nodded in unison. "They won't be much help, but their knowledge will be useful. We don't know cats. They do. If we help them, it'll make things better for us."

Ever curious, Mia questioned, "What does 'helping them' mean?"

"We're going to get rid of Raven," Layla rumbled deep in her chest. There was venom in the big black dog's response.

The predatory feline plagued the compound for years. So, Raven's attack on Mia was far from their first encounter, but Layla never had the freedom to do anything about the heinous cat. Now the resolute Sloughi could roam and hunt as she pleased.

"You can stay here. You don't have to be involved. Either of you." Layla looked at the battered bodies of the tripod and the grey dog.

Brodie puffed out his bruised chest and raised his head as high as it would go, making his response to Layla's statement clear.

Mia stayed silent. She was desperate to remain a valuable member of the pack, but the thought of facing off against another cat made her shake with fear.

"It's okay, Mia. You don't have to be brave this time." Ami's gentle reassurance helped a little, but the small dog remained troubled.

Mia quietly followed as Layla walked back into the bedroom.

"We want our house back." Layla began bluntly with her proposal to the apprehensive bed-dwellers. Nervously, the felines waited for the imminent instruction to leave, but Layla continued. "We'll get rid of Raven. You can take over another house. Any house but this one. Deal?"

Unsure of how to respond, the cats exchanged glances.

"Deal." One cat, toward the back, answered loud and clear. Until that moment, he'd barely reacted and remained silent.

By the way the others looked at him, it seemed he was the moggies' leader. The large, orange, battle-worn male had a stern face and a presence that commanded respect, even from the hounds.

Layla addressed him directly. "How many are there?"

"Lots. Twice as many as we are." The gruff orange cat answered, pulling no punches. It would be a challenge to eliminate Raven, but the animal showed no reluctance at Layla's request.

The big tomcat knew what needed to be done as he and Layla continued to discuss the plan. It was simple: they would choose the right moment and launch an offensive against Raven's army. According to the leader cat, nightfall would provide their best opportunity.

Layla never, in all of her life, expected to lead a clowder of cats. With the uneasy alliance secured, the stoic Sloughi called to everyone, "Get some rest."

As dusk fell, tension rose. The strange squad didn't have much in their corner, and everyone was hungry, weak, and tired. With thoughts of the impending conflict on their minds, restfulness was difficult to achieve.

Mia, in particular, was extremely troubled. She wanted to be of use. She wanted to help, but she knew she couldn't fight. She would inevitably need a rescue if she tried, and Mia didn't want to be an encumbrance on an already overburdened pack. Her tormented thoughts were interrupted by hissing and growling - the sign Layla and the orange tomcat arranged to signal the start of the clash.

"Who's Raven fighting? You're all here, aren't you?" Mia asked one of the cats.

"It'll be one of her own. It happens every night. She makes an example of one of them to make sure the others know to obey her. This is how she controls them."

Unaffected by the group's anxiety, Layla queried, "Ready?" The Sloughi was almost excited about the battle to come.

With a nod from the orange cat, the three large dogs descended the stairs and galloped outside to the street. They stopped and faced the hissing cats, spaced a stride apart, so they blocked the road ahead. The catfight came to a premature end as Raven crept forward a few steps, positioning herself in the middle of the road facing the dogs.

Incredulous, Raven slowly swished her tail and uttered, "Do my eyes betray me?"

Layla wasn't interested in a conversation with the malevolent animal. "It's time for you to leave this place."

"Oh, is it now?" Raven smiled.

The black cat's hideous grin made Ami nervously shuffle her feet.

And that skittish energy didn't go unnoticed by Layla. The pack leader knew that if she let the feline talk too much, Ami and Brodie might lose their nerve. Brodie, in his innocence, and Ami, in her softness, would fall prey to Raven's highly skilled psychological manipulation.

"It's time for you to leave this place," Layla repeated. "The rest of you are invited to unite with us." Layla addressed the cats that crept out of the shadows to stand behind their leader.

The little greyhound watched the scene unfold from the doorway, feeling horribly useless.

Puzzled felines tipped their heads and considered the commanding black dog.

Raven cackled, "Join a bunch of raggedy dogs? Oh, good one. That's funny. That's really funny. Now, get out of my compound."

Raven brazenly pivoted and flounced away. She stopped when she noticed her minions' expressions, and the black cat spun her head back toward the doggie brigade.

Raven watched the cats filing out of the house to join their new canine companions. "What is this?" the feline hissed as she turned a tight circle to survey the scene.

The allied cats hid their nervousness as they took their place amongst the dogs. Layla couldn't help but smirk at the thought of what the standoff must look like to their bewildered opponents.

The orange cat stood further forward and repeated Layla's offer to his former compatriots. "Join us. You don't have to live this way. You don't have to live in fear. We don't live like that."

"Please! You barely live at all! Look at you! I've never seen such a sorry bunch of moggies in my life!" Raven angrily spat the words as her tail swished erratically. Then she focused on the cat that dared to speak in her presence. "I should have known *you* would do this, Jones. Didn't you learn the lesson I gave you when I opened your stomach? I shall have to teach it once again."

"Why don't you ask *them* what they want to do?" Layla interrupted as she tipped her head toward the gathered cats. Serenely, the Sloughi surveyed the crowd. Challenging Raven's leadership might provoke an attack, but Layla was ready to wipe that smug expression off her adversary's arrogant face.

"Enough! Do you realise how outnumbered you are?" the vexed animal shrieked.

Raven's outrage was music to Layla's ears. The confrontation visibly shook the diabolical cat.

"They've got dogs, Raven," one of the cats beside the furious feline whispered, but not quietly enough.

Layla let out an audible snigger, which led Raven to jump on the cat and pin it to the ground.

"Not one more word," Raven growled as she pressed claws into her well-meaning ally's flesh.

Under her breath, Layla murmured to the tomcat, "Why hasn't she attacked yet?"

"She's buying time. She's planning something," the orange tabby explained.

"Behind you! It's an ambush!" Mia jumped at the chance to help her team when she spotted a sneak attack, and the tiny dog screamed out the warning.

As soon as Layla turned her head toward the advancing horde, Raven gave the command, and the enemy on her flank sprinted forward to overtake the blindsided rebels.

"Left side front! Right side back!" Layla quickly called the order, and all obeyed. Everyone on her left side charged forward toward Raven's faction, and those on her right, toward the ambushers.

"Ami, Brodie, you head back!" The hounds obeyed and headed up the rear-facing charge. Layla made a beeline for Raven. The Sloughi wanted this fight over as quickly as possible because the longer it went on, the more chance Brodie or Ami would come to harm.

It was no surprise to Layla that Raven didn't lead her army. Instead, the four-legged overlord sprinted to the back of the enormous group of cats, hissing at them to attack the incoming animals.

As the two groups collided, Layla pushed deeper into the crowd, trying to advance on the cowardly black cat. Those who fought alongside Layla tangled with the first line of aggressors and shouted their support for Layla as she pushed through the chaotic battleground, throwing cats out of her way left and right.

When Layla broke through the backline, she glimpsed the swish of Raven's tail as the feline bolted around a corner and out of view. Layla growled in frustration, but she was immediately distracted by the sound of an ear-piercing scream. She headed back into the fray; Raven would have to wait.

Brodie and Ami had an easier time. Once the sneaky group of cats saw two large dogs in pursuit, almost half abandoned the cause. The cowardly cats dispersed as they found places to hide from the dogs, the other moggies, and Raven - as they knew exactly what happened to deserters.

Victorious, Brodie and Ami received an extra boost of confidence that renewed their determination.

Brodie barely felt his recent injuries as he lolloped along.

As Ami fought through the diminished crowd, she shouted to the spitting, hissing cats, "What are you fighting for?" She called out the words over and over as she deflected claws and dodged bites, trying to make sure she didn't accidentally attack one of their own.

Soon, all of the 'right side back' team began to shout Ami's words as they fought. The ferocity of the fight dwindled as the enemy faction seemed to lose steam. The battle slowed as more clashes ended, and the two sides came to a complete stop. As the cats that previously fled peeked out of their hiding places, an exchange of glances was enough to solidify the truce.

With that, Ami and Brodie turned to join their leader, followed by their cat comrades and Raven's newest defectors.

* * * * *

The orange cat was in trouble.

When the fighting had broken out, Raven gave specific orders to her lackeys, "Target that orange tomcat and bring him to me."

Jones was strong and fought two cats at a time, but he was exhausted. And when three more descended on him, it was too much to fight off. The big male hit the ground, pinned down by his attackers. As he felt claws sink into his soft belly, Jones closed his eyes and yowled in pain.

Suddenly, the weight of the three cats disappeared. Jones opened his eyes and rolled to his side as the big black dog threw one of his attackers in the air while she immobilised the other two. The first cat landed on its feet with a thud. The orange tomcat braced for another fight, but it didn't come.

The three cats, the strongest of Raven's henchmen, looked bewildered. They struggled to process what they had just witnessed:

A dog. Saving a cat.

A dog. Putting itself in danger. For a cat.

Still in an attack stance, Layla growled, "Why are you fighting for her?"

The hostile trio asked themselves the same question. They looked at their battered comrades and called for them to stop.

An uneasy calmness descended as Ami, Brodie and the rest of the cats joined the street stand-off.

"There are so many of us. There's just one Raven. None of you need to live this way. Without you, she is powerless." Jones spoke as he picked himself up and made his way to Layla's side. Blood dripped from the big tomcat's wounds with every step, but it was clear his words carried weight. Hopeful expressions replaced the fearful, anger-filled ones as the oppressed cats exchanged glances.

Layla knew it would take more than words to release their allegiance to the evil cat. Glancing at Ami and Brodie, Layla was relieved to see they hadn't suffered any serious injuries. "Ami, stay here and help them. Tend to the wounds. Brodie, you rest now."

"Where are you going?" asked her three-legged friend. He received no answer as Layla turned and ran off with a determined stride.

Despite her exhaustion, Layla searched street after street and house after house. The single-minded Sloughi couldn't even catch the nefarious feline's scent. She ran up and down the roads, stopping outside each house to check for the revolting, familiar smell.

Layla began to think Raven might have left the compound of her own volition when the dog suddenly spotted a small figure in the distant darkness. It moved erratically along the only road in the compound without streetlights, and Layla's eyes took a moment to adjust as she slowly made her way toward the wriggling figure. It was but a moment before Layla realised who it was. "Mia! What are you doing?" scolded the angry hound as she sprinted toward the anxious grey dog.

"Shhhh! She's in there! I tracked her!" the greyhound excitedly regaled. Mia watched the battle from the safety of the house until she'd seen Raven flee. And the determined little dog slipped away unnoticed to follow the villain.

Suppressing her involuntary reaction to the greyhound's disobedience, Layla relented and provided Mia with the validation she yearned for with a heartfelt, "Well done, Mia. Thank you."

It was more gratitude than Mia ever expected to receive from the dog she bickered, quibbled, and squabbled with for so long. Utterly elated, Mia felt like a proper pack member, through and through.

"Go back to the others now. I'll take it from here," the Sloughi quietly directed.

Mia began to trot away, but as soon as Layla entered the house, she stopped and turned back. There was no way Mia would desert her leader now. She waited at the entrance to the house, ears pricked up so she would be able to hear if she needed to rally help.

18

Layla felt a chill run down her spine as she entered the house. It was the same chill she felt when she encountered Raven after Mia's attack. She crept slowly from room to room, following the unmistakable scent. It was dark, and every shadow looked like a black cat. It put Layla on edge, and she found it hard to keep from flinching.

The stealthy Sloughi moved to where the scent was strongest. *Raven is in this room. Raven is watching me,* her senses screamed.

The element of surprise was not on her side, but Layla didn't care. Raven's reign ended tonight. Nothing would stop that.

The dog's amber eyes dropped to the cat-shaped shadow in front of her. Had Raven given up? *Why isn't she trying to hide?* Layla silently wondered. Without a word, the Sloughi moved a back leg out to ensure her speed in taking down the cruel cat. As she did, Layla felt sharp teeth and talons sink into her hide and begin to shred her skin.

Clever Raven stalked the dog from the moment she'd entered the house, and when the cat saw her opportunity to pounce undetected, she took it.

When Layla mistook the ornamental cat for a real one, Raven took her chance. She clamped onto the howling dog, doing as much damage as she could before she had to let go.

Layla spun in circles to dislodge the claws and teeth. It took three tries, but eventually, Raven lost her grip and ran. With her eyes finally adjusted to the darkness, Layla's gaze followed Raven's retreat. The cat had lost its advantage over the large black dog, and both knew it.

The ebony cat scrambled to find a place to hide out of sight, but Layla was hot on her trail.

* * * * *

"Layla. Laaaaaaaaayla." Mia worriedly tried to call her leader. It was something between a whisper and a shout; Mia didn't want to be heard by the feline she feared. Realising the futility of trying to be heard but not heard, Mia decided she needed help. She cautiously scampered toward home - back to Ami and Brodie.

As the street came into view, Mia couldn't quite believe her eyes. Everything was still. Peaceful. Serene. *Was that... a laugh?* she wondered in disbelief.

Mia trotted on, leaving a wide berth between herself and the nearest moggy. As she passed them, her eyes moved from cat to cat. Then the greyhound's jaw dropped open, and her eyes went wide in disbelief: Ami and Brodie lounged near the front of the house relaxed and contented.

"Mia! Where have you been? I thought you were asleep in the house. I was calling you!" Ami gently chided.

A little insulted that her pack member believed her so uninterested in the goings-on that she could go to sleep, Mia lightly boasted, "I followed Raven."

The words made Ami, Brodie, and Jones jump to their feet. Mia realised she would need to explain herself. And fast. "She ran to a house at the other end of the compound. To hide, I think. But I followed her the whole way while you were all fighting. What happened with that, by the way?"

"Mia! Another time. Carry on!" Ami's brisk tone and no-nonsense gaze put the hyperactive dog back on track.

"Well, Layla found me when she went looking for Raven, and I told her where Raven was, and Layla went into the house, and she's been in there a long time, and I heard a scream and commotion, and then it got quiet, and I called, but I couldn't hear anything, and then I came back to get you!" Mia rattled off as quickly as her tongue could roll the words out. The little dog sighed at the end of her tale and took a much-needed breath.

"Where?" It was all Brodie wanted to know.

Jones moved closer and repeated the dog's question.

Mia stepped back. The big orange tomcat was twice her size and had an intimidating presence. She looked at him for a moment, then began to run back up the road.

The canine-feline trio followed. The rescue party hadn't gone far when they all stopped in their tracks. All eyes searched the random pools of light cast from an odd lamppost here and there. In the distance, a dog slowly moved through the shadows. The stride was unmistakably Layla's, and the team strained to make out the distortion in the Sloughi's silhouette.

"No," Jones uttered the word in disbelief.

"It is," Ami confirmed what they were seeing.

"Oh my gosh." Mia was the last to weigh in as the black dog got close enough for them to distinguish Raven's lifeless body clamped between Layla's teeth.

A sense of unease skittered through the group. The brigade of cats that followed Jones shifted restlessly. Regardless of the truce, the image of a dead cat in a bloodied dog's jaws would not help strengthen the alliance.

Layla paused and looked around. Her glance met Ami's worried one, then Layla's gaze dropped to Jones.

Unflinching, the battle-scarred tomcat stood before the big dog.

Layla tossed the black cat onto the ground. "Get up."

Confused looks fell across the crowd as Raven slowly got to her feet. She stayed hunched down, close to the ground.

A deep breath whistled past Ami's lips. Relief coursed through the gentle brown dog, and she was thankful that Layla had not destroyed the fragile peace between the species.

The Sloughi put a restraining paw on the defeated cat.

Outrage palpable, Raven growled and glared into the crowd of defectors. "Traitors!" she hissed as her eyes fell to her former generals. Their glances skittered away.

Layla looked at Jones. "It's your choice."

Every eye pivoted toward Jones. He knew Layla would snap the neck of the humiliated cat with a single nod from him.

Jones observed the crowd. The cats accepted him as their benevolent alpha. The truce they'd achieved came through righteousness and virtue, not by fear or oppression. Decision made, Jones looked back at Layla and shook his head.

Immediately, the hound removed her paw and moved backward. Raven shot a hateful glance at her, but Layla's part in this was over.

"Raven."

The cowering black cat lost her fearsome façade and looked up at her orange adversary.

Stripped of power and position, there was no more reason for anyone to be afraid of the sad creature, and Jones decreed, "You have my pity. And my mercy."

Raven recoiled.

"Your reign is over. You are never to show your face here again. Get out."

Raven squinted at the cats she once called generals, but this time, they held her gaze.

The vanquished animal was so pathetic that years of enforced subservience and fear among her followers vanished instantly.

Failing to find an ally in the silently jeering crowd, the demoralised cat swished her tail and retreated. Raven looked back a few times as if she might consider an apology, but it never materialized. And soon, she was lost to the night, doomed to survive alone.

Once the black cat was out of sight, the jovial atmosphere returned. Burdens floated away, and a sense of normality returned to the compound's four-legged inhabitants.

"Thank you, Layla. Thank you all."

The black dog nodded at her feline friend.

"Will you be okay here?" True to her nature, Ami's concern focused on the wellbeing of the abandoned cats.

Confident, Jones smiled as he spoke, "We'll be just fine… now."

Joyful grins spread over the feline faces as they slowly dispersed throughout the compound. And not one of the cats returned to the home that belonged to the dogs.

"They're not so bad, those things."

Mia shot a narrow-eyed look at Brodie as soon as he made the statement. "Easy for you to say. You weren't shredded by one."

As the last of the cats crept out of view, the pack was alone again, and victorious elation faded as stark reality descended. The hounds originally returned to the compound with the hope of finding Lilian and Tom. Battle fatigue and melancholy swept over the dogs and bitter grief transformed each face. Even Layla, who rarely showed any emotion, was too tired to remain stoic. She dropped her head low and slowly slunk toward the empty, lonely house.

"What's that?" Mia gazed at the end of the road, squinting her eyes in an effort to focus.

Layla stopped and looked around at the little dog.

"Is that a cat? Is that Raven back again?" Mia squealed.

Brodie immediately quashed the little greyhound's panic with a nudge and a tut.

Nonchalantly, Layla's glance followed Mia's, and her head shot up.

She briskly trotted to the middle of the road and stared.

"It's not, is it?" Ami whispered in disbelief. The gentle Saluki barely uttered the words before their leader bound away.

Exhausted as she was, Layla galloped off at full speed, excitedly racing toward the oncoming lights of the approaching car.

Although none of them could match the black dog's pace, the others hurriedly followed, and they were close enough to hear Layla's frantic whines.

"I can smell them!" Brodie jubilantly yelled.

The moment Lilian stepped out of the car, she was bowled to the ground by her favourite dog. The overwrought woman wailed with happiness as she threw her arms around Layla. "The others! The rest of them! Are they there?" Lilian shouted to Tom as he bolted over to the wiggly bundle of intertwined human and dog.

Before he could deliver an answer, the rest of the pack were upon them, whimpering, frolicking, and licking their beloved mum and dad.

"My angels. I'm sorry. I'm so so sorry." Lilian repeated the apology over and over as she checked each of her dogs. She ran her hands over their protruding ribs and hips. She wept uncontrollably as she felt scars and cuts and scabs. Then she pulled them all together and hugged them as one.

"I always come back. I always come back," Lilian repeated the words she often uttered to her hounds when she returned from holidays and work trips. They had never had so much meaning before.

"Come on, let's go." Tom barely got the car door open before Ami jumped straight inside, swiftly followed by the others. As they drove away, the dogs watched the houses pass by, wondering what would become of the place.

As the car pulled out on the main road, Mia chirped, "Wasn't it a good idea I ha…"

"Well done, Mia. Well done," Layla praised.

With the commendation of her head dog secured at last, Mia, closely followed by Layla, Ami, and Brodie, began to slip into a deep, contented sleep. The LongDogs didn't know where they were going, but it didn't matter. They were safe and all together again.

As Brodie's eyelids grew heavy, he glanced up at Lilian, who turned around in her seat to watch over them all.

Happy tears, he thought to himself as he drifted off.

ABOUT THE AUTHOR

Although "The LongDogs" is fiction, the hounds in the story are utterly real and wholly loved. Each of their individual tales are mostly factual, and as their human mum, it is my great joy to share Layla, Ami, and Brodie's life stories.

If you'd like to know more about these remarkable hounds, please feel free to visit their individual Instagram accounts. These photogenic hams are always happy to pose for the camera. And if you'd like to sneak a peek at what I'm up to, find me at www.louisacrook.com.

Mia

Mia is my first fur-baby, and she came from a responsible family breeder in Bloemfontein, South Africa. She is a well-travelled, feisty girl who has no qualms about putting dogs three times her size in their place. This itty-bitty greyhound sits at the head of the pack but leaves the leadership responsibilities to Layla. Visit Mia on Instagram @medem_mia

Layla

Layla is my first rescue dog, and this beautiful Sloughi is the one that started it all. She is complicated, strong-willed, and frighteningly intelligent. Layla is the dog that all others listen to, and my dignified girl keeps new rescues in line. Her influence ensures a harmonious dynamic between all the dogs I bring home, whether they are permanent or temporary residents. Visit Layla on Instagram @laylaandami

Ami

Originally found along the road by a kind person, Ami was taken to a local vet clinic. This lovely girl was only meant to be a foster, but as soon as she and Layla met, the two became inseparable friends. And my sweet-natured Saluki became the second addition to our growing family of rescued animals. She is gentle and motherly, always taking nervous newbies under her wing to show them that they have nothing to fear. Visit Ami on Instagram @laylaandami

Brodie

Brodie joined the pack as another foster-fail while he recovered from injuries sustained when he was hit by a car. Neglected by the veterinary surgeon charged with Brodie's care, I stepped in and took responsibility for him. My audacious Azawakh has truly beaten the odds, going from not even being able to stand up by himself to bounding around the desert like he never even had four legs. He is brave, protective, and has an indomitable lust for life. Visit Brodie on Instagram @brokenbrodie.

Thank you so much for reading "The LongDogs." If you've enjoyed the story, please consider leaving a review. Your words may inspire others to enjoy Layla, Mia, Ami, and Brodie's story.

I'd also like to offer you something special - a digital photo scrapbook of Brodie and Ami's sweet romance. Visit me at www.LouisaCrook.com/romance to get your free copy of this unique supplement to "The LongDogs."

Best wishes,
Louisa

Printed in Great Britain
by Amazon